Lonesome Man

The Smith Brothers #4

Sherilee Gray

Editor: Karen Grove

Proofreading: Judy's Proofreading

Cover Design by Cover Couture:

www.bookcovercouture.com

This is a work of fiction. Names, characters, businesses, places, events, locales, and incidents are either the products of the author's imagination or used in a fictitious manner. Any resemblance to actual persons, living or dead, or actual events is purely coincidental.

ISBN: 978-1-0670738-7-9 (Print)

Chapter One

Libby

"This is not the job for you," my roommate said into her phone. "He likes the girl-next-door look, and the full girlfriend experience. That's not you, Fantasia." Jessica listened a few moments more. "I said no." Then she hung up.

"What was that about?" I asked, my gaze sliding to her and away from the new invoice from Clarence Medical that had just landed in my inbox.

Jessica scowled at her laptop, then sat back with a sigh. "Every year this guy...he lives in the mountains, like so remote you can only reach it by plane. Anyway, he has one of our girls go stay with him, sometimes up to a month."

I screwed up my face. Jess worked for a super-exclusive escort service, and it was her job to match the clients with women.

She chuckled. "Come on, he's a country bumpkin like you. You're gonna judge this guy, really? You used to live in the middle of nowhere. Surely you can sympathize?"

I shrugged. "Okay, yes, it can get lonely. I mean, I wouldn't hire someone to come and scratch my, um...itch, but no, I'm not going to judge this guy."

Jessica smirked. "He's young, hot, and by the end of their stay, whoever I send out there comes back broken-hearted and totally in love with the guy. He's sweet and funny and attentive, fucks like a champ and enjoys getting his woman off. They fight over who gets to go every year. This time, it's for only two weeks though, and honestly, I've contemplated doing it myself."

"You're serious?"

She nodded. "Hell yes. A two-week vacation away from the city, where you're treated like a queen and experience multiple orgasms? What's not to like? He's had a girl flown in every year for the last four years. So we know he's safe, fun, and you earn a shitload of money."

A weird hot feeling moved through me. Was I blushing? It felt like I was blushing. "How much money?"

"After our cut...enough for a deposit on a really fucking nice house," Jessica said with a grin.

"What kind of women does he like?"

"Soft. Bigger girls. Curves, lots of them. No gym bodies."

"What about me?" I blurted before I knew I was going to say it. I was exactly what she described, though, and I needed money, a lot of it—and fast. I could cover Dad's medical bills for another month, then Mom would be left to look after him and pay for it on her own. She couldn't do that. My mom suffered from severe anxiety, and where they lived, she couldn't go out and get a job, even if she were capable of doing it. If I didn't make some cash, and fast, they were going to be in serious trouble. I was already working two jobs while trying to fit in auditions.

Jessica's eyes widened. "What?"

"How hard can it be?"

"You want to stay with this guy, have sex with him...for money? You, Libby Brantford?" Jessica said in disbelief.

"You just said you'd thought about doing it. Why not me? I need the money, Jess, you know I do, and I've had a one-night stand before. How is this any different?"

"Your father doesn't deserve shit from you, Libs. Yes, sex work is good honest work. Shit, I've taken the occasional job myself, but that's because I don't get all hung up on that stuff. You're built differently. And you sure as hell shouldn't have to pimp yourself out for your asshole father."

She was right, but I wasn't doing this for him. I was doing it for my mom. "What choice do I have? Mom can't do it alone."

"You'd be with this guy, one-on-one for two weeks. You can't get up the next morning and leave, not without a plane."

"I'm an actress. It would be just another role, and you said yourself he's a nice guy, that he's safe." I was beginning to like the idea more and more. I was positive I could get some of the girls at the bar to cover my shifts—I did it for them all the time—and what I'd earn doing this job would more than cover any income I'd lose.

"Libs, come on, you can't be serious?"

"I'm telling you I can do this."

"No way."

"Will he expect me to do a bunch of, you know, sex moves? A striptease or some freaky stuff in bed?" I really hoped not. "I mean, I could still do it, if I had to. I'll just research like I would for any other role."

Jessica chewed her lip, her head tilted to the side. "No, actually, he doesn't usually like anything over-the-top. Like I said on the phone, he wants the girlfriend experience. He likes the girls to relax and be themselves, have fun with him. Which is probably why they all fall for the guy. He gets under their skin, makes them feel seen, cared for, but ultimately, he always sends them back. We've lost two girls that way. They quit as soon as they got home, wanting to find *the one*."

"That alone is reason enough not to send any of your girls, right? And I'm literally the girl-next-door type. I can do this, Jess. I can go there, have some fun, come home and forget it happened. All my financial worries will be over, and I got a vacation with a sexy guy to boot."

Jess shut her laptop and shook her head. "Libs, no. This gig is not for you."

I may not have a huge amount of experience, but I wasn't some prude. I'd had a friend at college who'd paid her way by doing sex work. She'd loved it and made a crapload of cash.

I needed that money. I just had to talk Jessica into it.

Chapter Two

Libby

The small plane tilted to the side as it lined up with the runway, a stretch of field that seemed way too freaking short to me. The pilot, a huge guy named Cash, who'd said very little the entire way, wasn't helping my nerves any.

Nope, the butterflies in my belly were off the freaking charts. *You need to get it the hell together.*

My *client* had changed his requirements from previous visits. This time he didn't just want the girlfriend experience, he wanted me to pretend I was his *wife*—a wife he planned to knock up. He wanted family vibes, affection, love, kisses, and lots of sex.

No, he didn't want me to dance for him or do freaky stuff in the bedroom, but for the next two weeks he did want me to pretend I was his.

He wanted me to walk off this plane and greet him as if I already knew him intimately. His time was precious. He treated himself to this experience once a year; the rest of that time he was alone. He didn't have the luxury of *getting to know yous* and wooing or whatever.

It would require a lot of role-play on my part, but I was

an actor who excelled at improv, which was how I finally got Jess to relent. I could totally do this. I could give him what he wanted. So no, when I saw him for the first time, I couldn't be shy or awkward, I had to be excited. This wasn't two people meeting each other for the first time, this was a reunion.

I clicked open the last file from Jessica, the one that I hadn't looked at yet. This one had the important details, like name, age, and a photo. I'd deliberately chosen not to look until now, so I wouldn't have time to talk myself out of it. There would be no backing out if I saw him and he wasn't my type or he didn't meet some preconceived ideas I'd formed. I couldn't risk doing that, but I was only human.

My type shouldn't and couldn't factor into this, which is why I chose to wait until there was no opportunity to change my mind. Plus, this was how improv worked, no time to prepare, to overthink and get myself in knots and screw things up. I worked better this way.

My ears popped as the plane turned almost all the way on its side. I bit back my shriek before Cash, thankfully, pulled out of the turn and began our descent. I slid my phone into my pocket so I could grip the safety harness as we flew at speed toward a field. I squeezed my eyes closed, then sucked in a breath as the wheels finally touched the ground and bounced along the runway.

The plane had barely stopped before Cash opened the cockpit door, jumped down, and rounded the nose of the aircraft. He hadn't turned the engine off, and the propeller was still spinning as he opened my door, unbuckled my seat belt, and lifted me down like a sack of potatoes, planting me on my feet. He then grabbed my bags and carried them to the side of the runway.

He strode back, while I looked around me.

"Stand over there, Ruth," he yelled over the engine noise. "He'll drive up once I'm back in the plane."

"Oh, okay. Thanks, Cash." Ruth was my nom de plume, not that Libby was super unique, but I didn't want to risk using my own name. In the brief it said he'd have another name for me while we role-played, which I guess I'd find out when I met him.

Cash's lips curled in a half smile, and he gave me a chin lift. I hustled out of the way as he got back in the cockpit, and I watched as he swung the small plane around, then headed back down the runway.

I quickly tapped on my phone screen to open it so I could get the guy's name—nothing happened. *Crap.* My phone was dead.

The far-off sound of a revving engine grew louder, and I lifted my hand to shield my eyes as a truck appeared in the distance, heading toward me.

Oh shit, here he comes. And now I had no idea what he looked like or even his freaking name.

Thankfully I did know that if he was wearing something black, or we were in bed, I was to be in character unless he indicated otherwise. When we weren't in play, it was up to me whether we did anything sexual. His brief also said he wanted to jump straight into it the first day, so I was prepared for that at least.

I didn't need his name. I could get by without it, right? I was his wife, I'd use an endearment. At least until I charged my freaking phone.

Taking a deep breath, I shoved down my nerves and let my character take over. I was a young woman separated for several months from the man she loved, now finally they were going to be together again. She can't wait to touch him, kiss him, just be with him. It wasn't hard to get into character.

I told myself my fear over the unknown was excitement, and I let the flutters in my belly, and the throb of my pulse, fill me with anticipation. I was a wife, overflowing with the joy of seeing the man I loved again after so long without him.

The truck stopped and the door opened.

He got out.

Holy fuck.

My mind went blank and my heart felt as if it stuttered to a stop in my chest before bursting back to life.

Oh fuck, I knew him.

Tucker.

Holy shit, it was Tucker Smith.

We'd been introduced through a program for home-schooled kids, and because of how isolated we were, with no cell or internet service, we'd talked over two-way radio every Friday for years, until I'd gone to college, then we'd mainly emailed, but there'd been the odd phone call as well. He'd been my best friend, my only friend, then as we'd gotten older...

My stomach churned and guilt slammed through me.

He'd never seen my face, not really. The one photo he had seen of me, I'd been looking down, my hair obscuring most of my face, but I'd seen him. I knew what he looked like, every chiseled inch of that handsome face.

My junior year of college, there'd been an article published online about his woodwork, how he was selling to some exclusive stores in the city and making waves from his remote homestead in the mountains. I'd teased him about it—and had fallen even more in love with him than I'd already been.

We hadn't talked in four years though. I'd pulled back—I'd ghosted him because I was a goddamn coward.

Now Tucker, *my* Tucker, was striding toward me, in the flesh, tall and built and utterly freaking gorgeous.

And yes, he was wearing a black T-shirt under his jacket.

My heart slammed into the back of my ribs and my knees went weak. His gaze did a sweep of me from head to feet and his lips curled up in a gorgeous smile. Would he be able to recognize me from that one shitty photo I'd sent him? Would he recognize my voice? We hadn't talked over the phone much after I went to college because the cell and internet services were patchy out here, but it was still possible.

My feet were moving before I knew what I was doing. I ran at him and jumped. He caught me, his low chuckle lifting goose bumps across my skin as he held me close.

For so many years I'd wondered what it would feel like to be in this man's arms. I wrapped my arms and legs around him. "Tuck," I said breathlessly. He was huge and muscled and smelled like pine and sexy mountain man. I needed to tell him who I was. I needed to tell him the truth—

"Libby, baby," he said roughly, one hand on my ass, the other sliding into my hair. "You're finally here, darlin'."

The sound of a record scratching filled my head. *Libby? Did he just call me Libby? Yes. Yes, he freaking did. He knew who I was. Oh god, he knew it was me.*

He fisted my hair lightly, while my mind spun wildly. I lifted my head. His green eyes met mine, glittering, filled with pleasure, with heat. "Missed my little wife," he said.

My breath caught and my stomach sank. He looked

right at me without a scrap of recognition, and it was as if I'd been punched in the chest.

He had no idea who I was. He was playing a part, my husband—and he'd chosen Libby, *my name*, as the name of his fictional wife.

Holy fuck.

He wasn't forcing me closer, but he wanted it. He wasn't going to force anything if I wasn't into it, even though I was bought and paid for.

He was waiting, so I did what any wife would do, what I'd desperately wanted to do since I was thirteen years old—what any woman would, faced with a husband this beautiful and missing him badly—I kissed him. I wrapped my arms around him tighter and kissed the hell out of him.

I kissed Tucker Smith.

My Tucker.

He spun, pressing me against the side of the truck, his mouth opening over mine. His beard tickled as his tongue swept inside my mouth, and he tasted like peppermint and hunger, and I was instantly turned on. I'd imagined this moment for years, but this felt, god, so dirty and sexy and freeing.

Did this feel dishonest? Yes, but he never had to know it was me. He could never know it was me. Tucker had used my name, he'd called *me* his wife. He was pretending *I* was his wife.

I could never go back to living this kind of life, so secluded, which was why I'd pulled away when he asked me to come and stay with him several years ago, why I'd convinced myself I wasn't in love with him when he asked me to give this thing between us a go. But he didn't want anyone permanent, either. Right? That was why he did this. That's why he stuck to escorts now.

If he knew it was me, everything would get complicated, messy. Not only would it embarrass him, but I wasn't sure he'd even want to see the real me, not after the way I ended things between us. He'd brought someone out here to be with him because he wanted a fantasy, not the real Libby.

This was all we could ever have had, and by some miracle the universe had found a way to give it to me, to us.

The kiss deepened, and I focused on why I was here. I was here for him, so he could take pleasure from me. No one would ever know what we did together. I'd be gone in two weeks, then I'd never see him again. I didn't need to agonize over leaving him, or feel guilty about messing with his emotions. I could let all the walls drop. I could be with him, love him like a wife would, and feel no guilt and no shame.

His grip on my ass tightened, and he pressed against me, grinding his hard cock between my spread thighs. It was insane, but I wanted him, right then, so fucking badly. "I need you," I said against his lips. "I need to feel you inside me."

A shudder went through his big body. "Fuck," he groaned. "You deserve better than to be fucked against the side of the truck, Libs, but I can't wait to have you."

Libs. My heart crashed against my ribs.

We'd been in each other's company for two minutes and I was so hot for him, my panties were soaked. "Your wife wants to be fucked by her husband. That's what I deserve," I said, not sure where my courage came from, but the anonymity was so incredibly freeing.

He shuddered again, his hand gripping my bare thigh. His skin was rough as hell, and for some reason that turned me on even more. I dropped my legs long enough for him to yank my underwear off and shove them in his pocket.

He slid his fingers over my bare pussy.

"So fucking wet," he groaned.

"You do that to me," I rasped, not shy, not awkward, just needy as hell for him. Knowing it was just him and me out here, that I could let this happen and it was safe, god, it was liberating.

I yanked on his belt, undoing it quickly, then popped the button and hurriedly tugged down his zipper. He hoisted me back up, and I wrapped my legs around him again, while he kissed me wildly, just like desperate lovers reunited. Then the head of his bare cock was right there at my opening. He was thick, so much so that when he started pushing inside me I gasped for breath.

"Holy shit, Tuck, you're so big." I whimpered. "I missed this so much," I added, because I was his wife and this was our reunion, not our first time. He slid deeper. "*Oh fuck.*"

Tucker Smith was inside me. How was this happening? How was this my life? I felt like I'd won the goddamn lottery.

"You missed your husband's cock, didn't you?" he muttered against my lips.

My pussy spasmed. "Yes, I missed you so much," I said, thighs shaking. He was fucking huge everywhere. I'd never had a cock that big inside me and there was a pinch of pain from the stretch, but nothing I couldn't handle, and honestly, he felt so impossibly good.

I'd never been fucked without a condom before, either, but that was part of the wife experience he'd asked for. He wanted it raw. So I'd been tested and gone on the pill, and I loved that too. Loved that I got to play out this fantasy with him, because it was mine as well, wasn't it? All of this was my fantasy too.

He slid out and thrust back in, fucking me hard, like a

guy who hadn't been inside a woman for an entire year. I didn't expect him to last long, and I could tell he wasn't going to, not with the way he trembled, not with how he was now slamming into me, pinning me against the cold steel of his tuck, not when I was so close to coming myself from just this.

I never came from sex alone, but everything about this—seeing Tucker for the first time face to face, the role-play, being fucked by him—it was wrong and dirty and sexy as hell. My pussy spasmed, clamping down hard. I threw my head back, and his big hand was there, protecting it, as I orgasmed, crying out, pulling him with me while I sucked and kissed his gorgeous lips.

"Fuck," he growled. "That's it, Libby, come for me. Come all over my cock like a good little wife."

That's exactly what I'd just done.

He grunted, then groaned low as he slammed into me, pulsing heavily, pumping me full of come, holding himself deep, thrusting and grinding, while I panted and gasped for breath.

Finally, he lifted his head and kissed me deeply, then gentling slowly, making my head spin. "That was fucking perfect, Libs."

His praise made my belly swoop. I smiled up at him and hoped my lips weren't as trembly as they felt. I knew what he was saying, without him having to break character. I'd done good. I'd given him what he wanted. No, there was no way I could say who I was, not now. "Was pretty good from where I'm standing as well," I said, unable to stop looking at him, at that handsome face. How many times had I imagined being here with him? Too many.

He chuckled, pressed a kiss to my forehead, and slid out of me carefully. His come gushed out of me, sliding down my thigh when he lowered me to my feet. I looked down and Tucker did the same. When I looked back up, my face heated for some stupid reason, but he made a low, growly sound.

He liked seeing his come on me. He took my panties from his pocket, then stunned me by crouching and using them to clean me up before putting them back in his pocket.

He straightened, then gently eased me forward and opened the truck door for me. "Let's get you home. It's getting cold."

I bit my lip and nodded, climbing in. He closed the door behind me, then strode over to collect my bags. I couldn't believe I'd just had sex with him. With Tucker. Four years ago, he'd still been my best friend, my dream guy, my hot-as-hell mountain man, who I wanted so badly I ached, but who would forever be out of reach for so many reasons. So no, I didn't feel used or weird despite the fact that he'd paid for it, that he'd paid for me. Rather, I felt warm all over—excited to be here with him. Yes, there was a little bit of guilt, but it wasn't like I'd planned this.

He strode back, put my bags in the bed of the truck and got in, then glanced over at me. "Made your favorite for dinner."

"You did?"

He nodded, started the truck, and we headed off.

I'd answered a questionnaire several weeks ago that asked me all kinds of things about myself. Including my favorite meal, what else I liked to eat. My favorite scent, flower, TV shows, music. I'd been given the same info about him, that part of the brief I had read, but still, nothing had tipped me off. How could it? I never in a million years thought I'd get off that plane and find Tucker waiting for me. "Good, 'cause I'm starved."

He glanced over at me again, his gaze sliding down my body. "Me too."

His voice was deep and rough, and there was no missing his meaning. Tucker was going to make the most of his time with me, and I was more than happy with that. My nerves had settled, not surprising. Sex was a serious icebreaker. The intimacy side of this was going to be harder for me, though, especially now, but whatever happened over the next two weeks, I couldn't allow myself to completely fall for this man.

So when he said, "Come 'ere," in that sexy voice of his, my nerves burst back to life, and I did what he asked and slid across the bench seat and pressed into his side. He wrapped his arm around my shoulders, and I was finding it hard to breathe normally again.

We drove over a rise and the house came into view. It was breathtaking, a two-story with walls made of thick logs stacked on top of each other, and there was a wide wrap-around porch that surrounded the entire house. A large barn stood beside it as well as a few other smaller outbuildings.

I nearly said how beautiful it was, but I stopped myself. We were still in play, so I'd already know what it looked like.

Tucker pulled to a stop. "Wait there." He got out and rounded the hood again, opening the door for me. "Head inside, baby, I'll get the bags."

I nodded, pressed my hand to his chest and looked up at him. He leaned in and kissed me, making a humming sound of contentment when he did. It was so remote out here; we were literally in the middle of nowhere. I knew how lonely a life like this could be, but he was totally alone now that his parents were gone. An awful churning filled my belly, while memories of the past, of my childhood tried to force their way forward. I quickly shoved them down before they could take hold. No wonder he did this. He used to play the loneliness off when we talked, that he liked the peace, but going without physical contact for so long, he had to be craving another human being, just someone to talk to, a simple touch. A hug.

My heart clenched, hurting for him.

I headed inside while he grabbed the bags and followed. A fire crackled in the living room. It was warm and cozy, and I loved it.

"Dinner smells amazing."

"I did the potatoes the way you like. Come on." He reached for my hand and led me upstairs and into what was obviously his bedroom.

The bed was intricately carved wood, the rest of the furniture was the same. It smelled fresh in here, with a hint of vanilla, my favorite scent. "You wanna grab a shower? There's time before the food's ready."

"Yeah, that'd be great," I said, trying not to let the awkwardness sink in.

He strode over to me, his strong hands curling around my upper arms. "Really fucking glad you're here, Libs," he said, voice husky.

It was another thing that a husband would say to his wife after time apart, but I knew it was the real woman under the fantasy he was talking to. That it had come from a place of deep loneliness, and he meant it. "Me too," I whispered.

He'd wanted me as much as I had him, and he had no idea that the real Libby was standing in front of him, that it was the real Libby he'd just kissed.

Chapter Three

Tucker

RUTH WAS STRAIGHT OUT of my deepest fantasies.

Smith men liked their women soft and curvy, and my girl was so hot it had been a fucking challenge leaving her to shower alone. But I was raised right, and that beautiful, sweet-as-candy woman had just traveled hours, taken two flights to get to me, and I was going to feed her before I fucked her again.

Still, my hands actually trembled as I dished up the pot roast and warmed up the gravy. I put down the ladle and shook out my hands. This was a lot, it always was. I hadn't seen another soul in three months, the last time Cash visited, and I hadn't been with a woman in over twelve. Now Ruth was finally here, looking like my wildest dreams, playing the part of my Libby, the only girl I'd ever allowed myself to fall for, and I needed to get a fucking handle on it.

I'd had women out here once a year for the past four years and I'd never felt this kind of instant connection before. I'd definitely never fucked one of them within two minutes of meeting them, and I wasn't sure it was her or because of who I was pretending she was. When Jessica sent Ruth's photo, I'd been fucking struck. She'd been everything I'd wanted, exactly how I'd pictured Libby, and now she was here and even more perfect in the flesh.

Footsteps echoed on the stairs as she came back down from the bedroom. "Hope you're hungry?" I said. "I made extra grav—"

Her warm, soft body pressed against my back, her arms coming around me. "I'll need extra everything, please," she said and laughed.

I let out a shuddery breath. This girl knew the fucking assignment. Jesus, she had me off-balance. I was still wearing black, so she was still playing her part, and I wasn't sure I ever wanted my little wifey to break character. I liked this too fucking much.

She released me and walked to the fridge. "Beer?"

"Yeah, please."

We sat and ate and drank and I was having trouble looking away from her.

"What do you want to do after dinner?" she asked, her eyes lifting to mine and her cheeks turned pink.

My little wife blushed often. It was a surprise, but I fucking loved that too. "You," I said.

Her lips curved up, and she nodded as she sipped her beer. "Right answer."

"Yeah?" I swallowed, the sound loud in the quiet kitchen.

"We have a lot of time to make up for," she said, lowering her knife and fork.

Some people might think I was fucked in the head, doing this—role-playing this way, pretending this total stranger was the love of my life—especially since Libby, the real Libby, actually existed. Some might even think I was sad or desperate or weird. I didn't give a fuck. You paid a price, living the way I did. The solitude, the loneliness, it cost you. I craved love and affection like anyone else, but the chances of me ever finding it while living out here were slim to none. That's why Libby had stopped emailing me and why she refused to answer my calls. That was why she'd drifted away. She'd told me over and over while we were growing up that she hated living the way she did, but I'd pushed for her to come here, to be with me anyway. I couldn't give her what she wanted, though. She'd had feelings for me, but she'd also made it clear, living this way wasn't something she'd ever do again.

My cousins had lucked out, but they didn't live as far from civilization as I did. The truth was, no woman would give up everything to be out here with me, so I did this once a year, I gave myself this.

Only this year, I'd taken it one step further. For two weeks, I wanted to know what it was like to be someone's husband, to be Libby's husband. Role-playing I was with her was a kind of goodbye, I guess. I had to let the fantasy of me and Libs being together go, for my own good, and honestly, for my mental health. Living out the fantasy was my way of doing that.

I reached out and cupped the side of her face, sliding my thumb over her full lower lip, my heart thumping hard. "You miss me, baby?"

She lifted her hand, covering mine. "Like you wouldn't believe." She stood, and I slid my seat back so she could climb into my lap. She pressed her body into mine, her mouth going to my ear. "I'm ovulating," she said huskily.

My heart thumped harder in my chest. *Oh fuck.* Yeah, she understood the assignment all right. The fantasy of Libby, my plump little wife, begging me to fuck her, to put a baby in her, of fucking like rabbits to knock her up, hadn't let go. And it wasn't going to, not until I let myself have it. "You want me to put a baby in you, darlin'?"

She pressed her full tits against my chest. "Yes," she whispered. "I hope you had your vitamins this morning, honey, because if it's gonna take, we'll need to do it a lot."

"You had enough to eat?" I asked, my voice rough as hell.

"Yes."

I stood, lifting her with me, and strode through the kitchen and up the stairs. What I wanted to do was lay her on the table and eat her pussy, but I'd already fucked her against my truck, and I could see she was tired, so this time I was fucking her in my bed.

I carried her into my room and laid her on the mattress. "You want me to eat your pussy first, Libs?"

The pulse at the side of her throat was fluttering wildly. She licked her lips. "Yes...please."

I slid my thumbs down the sides of her shorts, dragged them down her legs slowly, and tossed them aside. She wore pale blue panties, plain, not lacy or a G-string, nothing trying to be overtly sexy, but somehow they were the sexiest thing I'd ever seen. Sliding my hands up her calves, spreading her thighs, I kissed the inside of her knee. Looking up, I pressed my thumb against her pussy, rubbing her over her panties, and groaned when I felt how soaked they were. Fuck, I needed this, I needed a taste of my girl.

Tearing them down her legs, I buried my face against her pussy with a low moan. She was smooth and soft, so fucking hot, and Christ, wet as hell. Holding her spread wide for me, I licked and sucked her, and fuck me, she tasted incredible. It was hard, but I didn't grind against the mattress like I desperately wanted to. If I did, I'd come before I got inside her. Sliding my thumb over her slick little clit, I indulged myself, slipping my tongue inside her before finally gripping her hips, yanking her closer, and sucking her clit into my mouth as I thrust two fingers inside her.

She arched on the mattress with a cry, her thighs shaking as she came hard for me, her inner muscles clutching at my fingers repeatedly.

I kissed her pussy one more time, then straightened and tugged off my shirt, then yanking open my jeans, I shoved them and my boxer briefs off as well. Her gaze moved over my naked body, lingering on my cock, and she licked her lips. Yeah, I liked that too. She was open, different than the girls I'd had here in the past. When they first arrived, it took a couple days before they realized I gave a fuck about their pleasure as well, and they'd fake shit, smiles, laughter, orgasms.

Ruth wasn't giving me that. Even while we role-played there was this genuine warmth, almost affection in her eyes, and there was no hiding how much she wanted me. You sure as fuck couldn't fake the way that pussy was dripping. "Take your shirt off, darlin', want to see your tits when I fuck you."

She nodded and quickly stripped off, her cheeks flushing a darker pink. Why was that fucking with me so much? The blushing. But it was. I loved it. She was exactly what I'd want, exactly how I'd imagined Libby would be. Christ, how she'd look. If this was real, if I could have this, she was exactly what I'd want. A curvy, soft little wife who blushed when I said dirty shit. Who missed me when we'd been parted, so much so, she let me fuck her against my truck, and who had a tight-as-fuck pussy that tasted like pure ecstasy.

Her tits were big and round, gorgeous, the nipples peach colored and tight. I climbed onto the bed between her curvy thighs, leaning down to kiss her rounded, soft belly, across her ribs, then gripping one of those soft tits, I sucked a puckered nipple into my mouth. She made a strangled sound and fisted my hair. "Oh...*oh, shit.*"

Again, the sounds she made were real, raw. There was no practiced porn monologue, something else I'd gotten in the past, until they realized I got off on making them feel good as well, that I wanted them to have as much fun as I did while they were here. Ruth had already gotten the memo. Fuck it was hard to think of her as anyone but Libby, that's how good this girl was. I was already so deep in the fantasy.

Hard not to be when it was obvious she wasn't faking how I made her feel. Every gasp and whimper was real, and it was making me lose my mind.

I lifted my head and leaned in, kissing her full, rosebud mouth, covering her body with my much larger one. I'd sent a list of my kinks, but it'd been so long since I'd been with a woman, since I'd been able to indulge, it usually took me a couple days to warm up. Not this time, not with Libby. My little "wife" made me fucking feral. "Are you going to be a good girl for me?" I rasped, voice hoarse as fuck.

She blinked up at me with those big, green eyes, more pink hitting her cheeks as her throat worked with her rapid swallows. "Y-yes. I'll be a good girl."

I squeezed, then tugged on one of her nipples, wringing a gasp from her. "Only good girls get fucked hard, but only very good girls get pumped full of come. Are you a very good girl?"

She nodded. "Yes... I'll be very good."

I pressed the head of my cock to her opening. "Gonna fill this pussy, over and over, until you're full of my come, Libby." I pushed inside her, just an inch.

"Please...I want it," she gasped out. "I want that."

"Yeah, you do," I growled as I slid deeper, hissing at how tightly she gripped me. "Gonna fuck you so hard, over and over until I put a baby in you, little wife," I said, letting fantasy take a stronger hold, letting myself sink into my most secret longing as I thrust deeper into my Libby.

"Shit," she said, panting. "Holy fuck."

"You gonna let me destroy this pretty pussy? You want it hard, don't you, Libby?"

"Yes...god, yes." Her nails dug into my back. "I want it."

Groaning, I slammed my hips forward, then proceeded to fuck her so hard, air was forced from between her pouty lips every time I filled her. I wasn't going to last long. Yes, I'd fucked her once already, and not that long ago, but it'd been a long fucking year, and this woman, this fantasy, was too good, too real. Maybe it was twisted, but to me she *was* Libby. She was my fucking Libby, and she was perfect.

I ground down as I filled her like a pussy-drunk madman. She arched against the mattress, her mouth falling open. "Let me feel it. Come around my cock, Libby. That tight-as-fuck little pussy is too good, you're gonna make me come, I want you to take it all. Fucking take it, Libby," I groaned.

She screamed, her pussy clamping down hard around me a second before I started coming. Her pussy milked me, gripping me over and over, feeding my fantasy. "You feel that?" I gasped. "You're pulling my come so deep inside you, little wife." I moaned, overcome by what I was feeling. Fuck, every moment had been perfect. It was dirty, sexy, beautiful. Libby was a dream under me, every bit of her exposed skin flushed pink, eyes satisfied and heavy, lips puffy and dark—pussy tight as hell, and now messy as fuck.

I collapsed against her, breathing hard, and while we both tried to catch our breath, she rubbed my back.

When I finally slipped out of her, I slid down the bed a little, holding her legs wide. I wanted to see my come inside her, and I groaned again when it started to slide out. Catching it with my fingers, I pushed it back in. She whimpered, her belly trembling. "Fuck," I muttered. "That's so fucking sexy, Libs, but you need to take it all," I said and scooped it up again, pushing it in a second time. "You need to keep your husband's come inside you, don't you, baby."

It was too good, too real, and I wasn't ready for the fantasy to end, not yet.

She looked down at me, eyes still heavy, biting her lip and nodded. "I want it. I want all of it."

"That's my good girl," I said, slowly pumping my fingers in and out of her come-filled pussy. "You're doing so fucking good." I looked up at her, holding those gorgeous eyes. "I'm gonna fuck you, baby, so many times, and I'm not gonna stop until it takes."

She shivered, giving me another gorgeous fucking blush. "I want that too."

I sucked in a sharp breath.

Jesus fucking Christ.

This woman was perfect.

Chapter Four

Libby

WHEN I WOKE I was in the bedroom alone. Music played quietly downstairs and the smell and sounds of cooking drifted up from the kitchen.

I stretched, then shivered when I felt the subtle aches in my body. I'd never experienced anything like I had last night with Tucker. The things he said, Jesus, I'd never been more turned on in all my life. I'd never come that hard either. How the hell would I survive two weeks? Two weeks of dirty, sexy Tucker giving me insanely good orgasms and the kind of sex I'd only ever fantasized about. I never thought I'd be into anything kinky like this, especially role-playing or breeding fantasies, but I was... Shit, it was so hot.

This whole thing was beyond confusing. I was an actor, I was playing a role—but pretending to be Tucker's wife was definitely no hardship. Not at all. I didn't have to fake my enthusiasm at being with him, because I'd wanted this, to be with him like this, for so damn long. Getting all caught up in this fantasy would be a mistake though. I had to regulate my emotions and, whatever it took, not let my heart get carried away.

It'd be so easy to dwell in my guilt, but I couldn't do that either. It wouldn't be fair to Tucker to tell him the truth, not now. Not when nothing had changed, and the reasons we couldn't be together beyond this still existed.

God, over the years we'd meant so much to each other. We'd been best friends; he'd been my only friend for a long time. He'd work on silly stories all week to tell me during our Friday calls just to make me laugh. Then when I went to college, the occasional call, and the long emails he'd sent telling me how much he missed me, and the last one, when he'd asked me to come and see him, to take a chance on him, to finally see if this thing between us was as real as it felt...

I'd known then, what I absolutely knew now—yes, it was real. Being here with him made it clear just how compatible we were in every way. If I'd come here four years ago, I would have fallen even harder for him. I would have stayed here, and eventually, I would have resented it. I would have resented him. So I told him I wasn't ready for what he wanted and that we needed to cool it for a while—then I'd ghosted him, like a fucking coward, afraid if I gave him another shot, if I let him, he'd talk me around and I'd give in. I'd give everything up for him, everything that I'd worked so hard for.

So no, I could never tell him who I was. Not after that, not after what I did to him to protect myself.

I was here now. By some fluke, some twist of fate, I was here with Tucker, like he'd wanted. So I could dwell on the past, or I could enjoy the time I had with him. I would make this perfect for him and try not to overthink it.

He still wants you.

And I still wanted him. But two weeks was all I could allow myself.

Pushing back the covers, I climbed out of bed and hit the bathroom. After a quick shower, I tied my hair back and dressed. My stomach growled and fluttered with nerves at the same time as I took the stairs and walked into the kitchen.

Tucker stood at the counter, dishing up whatever it was he'd cooked. By the smell of it, bacon. He was shirtless, in only a pair of gray track pants. His back was muscled and smooth, well, except for the pink lines across it I'd made with my fingernails.

No black.

We weren't playing this morning. My nerves shot higher. Role-playing some made-up version of myself was so much easier than reality, especially with him.

He put the pan down and turned, his perfect lips, surrounded by that sexy beard, curving when he saw me. His green gaze flicked down my body, taking in my bare legs and shorts, then the soft hooded sweatshirt I'd pulled on, then finally, my makeup-free face. He said in his brief that he liked bare skin or only a little makeup and so did I, which made things easier.

He walked across the kitchen and pulled me into his arms, wrapping me in a mountain-man bear hug. "Morning, Ruth," he said, using the false name I'd given.

Could this get any more complicated? My real name was my "fake" name, and as far as Tucker knew, my fake name was my real name.

"Morning," I said, running my hands up and down his bare back, while my face heated and I told myself over and over not to be weird or awkward now that I had to be *myself,* though this was more of an act than when we were role-playing. It was cold outside, a light dusting of snow on several of the mountain peaks in the distance, but his skin was hot.

"You sleep okay, darlin'?"

"Yeah, really good," I said, sounding all breathless.

He lifted his head, his hot, rough-skinned hands going to either side of my face. "Yesterday... Christ, last night, it was fucking perfect." He grinned. "You did so good, darlin'. Made my fucking year."

His tone was different now, some of his intensity gone.

He searched my eyes, rubbing my back. "Things were pretty intense, huh?"

I nodded. "Yeah," I said, my belly going all squirmy.

"You okay with everything?"

This was my Tucker, sweet and kind and gorgeous. Seeing this little show of uncertainty from him, making sure I was okay, washed my nerves away, and all I wanted to do was put him at ease. This was my chance to give him *me*, to give him his Libby, even if he never knew the truth. I smiled up at him. "Yes, absolutely."

"I was so excited to see you, and you were just so fucking perfect, Ruth, I lost my head." He gave me another devastatingly handsome grin. "I didn't even tell you anything about the house or the property, but I really want you to enjoy yourself while you're here. I don't want you to think of this as work. I want you to think of this as a vacation...with a fuckload of orgasms. But if you're not in the mood, or you're sore or whatever, we'll do something else, yeah? Though, I gotta say, you're probably the most beautiful woman I've ever laid eyes on, so keeping my hands to myself won't be easy."

I blinked up at him, my face heating again. "No... I'm not..." I laughed awkwardly. "You don't have to say—"

"Not feeding you a line, darlin'. Don't need to. The

beauty of this arrangement is that we can both completely let go, no bullshit, even when we're role-playing, because even then, what I say to you, I mean." His hands slid down to my hips and he squeezed, making me suck in a breath. "This face," he said, brushing his thumb along my jaw. "The hair, those lips, this...fuck, this body," he said, giving me another squeeze. "It was like you were plucked out of my fantasies and delivered right to my mountain. No, I will never, ever force you to do anything you don't want to, but know, I really fucking want you, and if you're into it, I'll indulge myself like a kid in a fucking candy store while I have you here."

My face got even hotter, and he chuckled, brushing the backs of his fingers over my cheek. "Really like the way you blush all the time."

"It's a curse," I rasped, still recovering from what he'd just said. He was making it clear he wanted me to be just as into him as he was me, as if he hadn't gotten that point across from the moment I arrived. But he was right, I didn't have to try to impress him or wonder if we were right for each other, that's not what this was. In the spirit of that, I decided to be just as open with him, at least as far as my attraction to him went. "Oh, I'm into it. You are..." I chewed my lip. "Gorgeous, and if we're talking about fantasies, you could have been plucked out of a few of mine as well." I'd had more fantasies about this man than he'd ever know. "Sexy, huge mountain man all to myself? Yes, please." His smile widened, and I couldn't hold back my own, or stop my stupid hot cheeks that were probably glowing right now. "Honestly, last night was the best sex I've ever had."

His smile slipped a little. "I'm not feeding you lines, Ruth, don't want you to either."

I held up my hands. "I'm not feeding you a line. I never

come like that, not without a whole lot of foreplay, definitely not from sex alone." I shrugged. "I don't know what it is." *Yes, you do. It's him. It's all him.* "But you make me feel at ease, safe, I guess, and being out here..." I shrugged again. "Like you said, there's no need to bullshit."

He stared down at me, his gaze searching mine, then he licked his lower lip, not trying to be seductive, but it just was. Everything about him was. I still didn't think he believed me, though.

He thought I was a sex worker. "A lot of sex doesn't necessarily mean good sex," I said.

He nodded. "That's true."

"Not that I've had *that* much sex," I said for reasons unknown. I mean, it didn't matter how many partners someone had. I didn't care, and obviously Tucker didn't, but I wanted him to at least know one thing about me that was true.

His brows shot up. "No?"

That was probably the wrong thing to say, though, considering why I was here. Shit. "I mean, compared to some, I haven't had that many, um...clients before you. I'm picky, I guess."

He kind of stiffened. "Yeah? I assumed you'd been doing this a while..."

"Jess wouldn't have sent me if she didn't think I was the woman for the job." I laughed, and it sounded a little strained even to me. "Do you have any complaints? If so, please report them to HR," I said in a silly voice, then blushed *again* because I was a fucking idiot.

Luckily, his smile returned, full wattage. "Definitely no complaints."

"Glad to hear it. Now, I assume that breakfast is for me? It smells freaking amazing, and as usual, I'm starved."

He steered me toward the table. "Then sit, woman, and let me feed you."

Tucker put a large plate of food in front of me, made us coffee, then joined me at the table.

"Like I said, I want you to make yourself at home, Ruth. While you're here, what's mine is yours. Eat what you want, when you want, go where you want. Nothing here is out of bounds, yeah?"

"Thanks, I'll do that," I said and quickly looked away when I found myself caught up in those gorgeous green eyes of his.

"So, how long have you been doing this?" he asked, and I felt his gaze burning into me as I took a fortifying sip of my coffee.

"Oh, only a little while. I'm an actor and a writer—in other words, a starving artist." I laughed. "I've known Jess a long time and got into escorting through her, um...last year."

"Yeah? An actor?" His Adam's apple slid up and down his throat at the mention of what I did.

Sharing real details about myself, within reason, wasn't a huge risk, because there is no way in a million years Tucker would think the real Libby was an escort, fake or not, even if we were both actors. "Yep."

"You been in anything I would have seen?"

"I do theater mainly," I said.

He looked down at his plate. "I have...had a friend who did theater in the city," he said, then looked up and there was pain in his eyes.

Had.

Had a friend.

He was talking about me. I'd put that pain there.

"What happened?" *Stop. Shut the hell up.*

He shrugged a broad shoulder and flashed me his beautiful grin. "I'm not all that sure to be honest, but it sucked." He chuckled. "Enough of my sob story. How about I show you some of the property after breakfast?"

"I'd love that," I said.

"Excellent. Then eat up, darlin', and we'll head off."

Chapter Five

Tucker

I HIT the bottom of the stairs, and Ruth turned to me, her pretty brown eyes moving down my body, taking in my boots, jeans, then finally my black T-shirt. Yeah, baby, it was time to play.

"You ready to have a little fun?" I said as I strode into the kitchen.

Her eyes lit up, and a wide smile spread across her face. "Always. What do you have in mind?"

I grabbed the basket from the pantry. I'd put together a picnic before I made breakfast. "Get out and enjoy the sunshine, then have some lunch at our favorite spot."

She came straight to me, wrapping her arms around my waist, and looked up at me. "Sounds perfect." Then she went up on her toes, and I leaned in, kissing her. *Fuck me.* My little wife was addictive. This was only day two and I was already fucking seriously into this.

It was hard, but I ended the kiss first, but only because I was *this close* to picking her up and laying her on the table. If I did that, we'd never leave the house, and I wanted Ruth...no, Libby, while we played, I was going to think of her as Libby. I wanted her to see the property, and I had plans.

I handed her a jacket, gloves, and hat. The sun was out, but it was cold, and there'd been a light dusting of snow on some of the surrounding mountains this morning. When she was all wrapped up, I took her hand. "Let's go, baby."

Her hand was warm in mine as I led her outside and over to the ATV. She got on without instruction, like she'd ridden one before, which surprised me. I strapped the basket on, climbed on as well, and started the bike. Libby slid forward and wrapped her arms around me, and I couldn't suppress my shiver when her soft, warm curves pressed tight against my back.

I let that sink in, that feeling of being wanted, of how it felt to have *my wife* show me easy affection. I dropped a hand, covering hers, then lifted her other one, pressing a kiss to her wrist, then put it back on my stomach and we headed off.

She hung on tight as we drove across the property, and I couldn't help but wonder if she liked my corner of the world. I loved it here, despite the loneliness. I planned on living my whole life right here, and I guess that was hard for some people to understand. This place was a part of me, though, it was in my veins and part of my soul, and I wanted this sweet, sexy woman hanging on to me, to see the beauty of it the way I did.

We rode for about thirty minutes, and when we stopped outside the little old cottage I'd been renovating, I heard her soft gasp as she jumped off the back of the ATV.

"Thought it was about time to show you my surprise," I said and winked.

She bit the side of her lip and smiled. "Wow, this place...it's beautiful."

"My grandparents used to live here. My father built our place, well, half of the lower level. I added on, built it up, making it a family home for us." I tilted my head toward the cottage. "My grandparents stayed here, though, their whole lives. You wanna take a look inside?"

"I'd love that."

I grabbed the basket and, taking her hand, led her inside. "I've been renovating it while you were away. It's been taking time since I have to get Cash to fly everything in." We were playing newlyweds, so there would still be things she might not know about her husband and the property. But since this was a fantasy, as long as we weren't thrown out of play, it didn't really need to make sense.

"What are you going to do with it?" she asked as I opened the door.

"I thought we could list it for rent, for short-term vacations, maybe a few times a year. Give people an experience, you know? Fishing, hiking, there's some amazing backcountry skiing around here as well. Cash will fly them in, we'll make sure the place is clean and stocked with food, and leave them to it or offer some guided tours around the area if that's what they want."

"That's such a great idea." She turned slowly, taking in the place. "It's so pretty, you've done an amazing job."

I headed to the fireplace in the living room. It was already stacked and ready to light, so I used the lighter on the mantel and got it going.

"It's also really romantic. This would be a great location for a honeymoon. No chance of interruptions out here."

I closed the space between us. "That's a good idea. A couple could fuck in every room in this house, they could walk around naked and no one will see, no one will bother them."

She licked her lips and nodded. "Maybe you should put that in your advertising?"

I chuckled. "It sure as hell would work for me." Fuck, I was hard as iron, and holding myself back was torture, but I was kind of getting off on the anticipation.

"Me too," she whispered.

Heat fired through me, and I had to stop myself from reaching down and adjusting my dick. "I'm so glad you're back, Libs," I said huskily.

"I missed you so much," she said, her eyes softening.

"How much?" I curled my fingers around the side of her throat.

Her lids fluttered, and she looked deep into my eyes. "So much I ached."

"Tell me where you ached."

She pressed her hand to her chest. "Here," she said, then slid her hand lower over her belly and gently cupped herself between her thighs. "And here."

Fucking hell.

I slid my hand up into her hair and fisted lightly. "Did you touch yourself while you were away from me?"

She nodded, licking her lips. "Yes."

"What did you think about while you played with your pussy, darlin'?"

She released a shaky little breath. "You." She took her hand from between her thighs and pressed it to my hard-as-fuck cock straining against the zipper of my jeans. "This." She gave me a squeeze, wringing a groan from me. "Hard, and thick, pushing inside me, thrusting into me."

I was going to come in my fucking pants if she kept that up. "Undo my jeans."

Her hands shook as she did as I ordered, tugging open

the button and dragging down the zipper, then her hand was curling around me, gripping me tight.

Sliding my thumb over her full, gorgeous, lower lip, I held her wide gaze. "On your knees, Libby. Time to show your husband how much you missed his cock."

Her cheeks were pink and her pretty lips parted on a breathy, needy sound before she did as I asked and dropped to her knees.

❄

Libby

I looked up at Tucker as I took his thick cock in my hand. He didn't touch me, just kept his hands at his sides. He was too long to take all of him, and when I sucked him deep into my mouth, he bumped the back of my throat.

Tucker watched me with hungry eyes as I started working his hard length. Swirling the tip with my tongue, I teased before forcing him as deep as he could go, and each time I sucked his cock deep, I worked my tongue along the smooth underside.

Tucker groaned, and I looked up at him, gripping his hips, and worked him faster.

His lips parted, panting, as I squirmed and squeezed my thighs together, getting turned the hell on seeing him like this.

"You're doing so good, Libs. You're my good girl, aren't you, darlin'?"

All I could give him was a subtle nod, but hearing his praise, having him call me his good girl, had me sliding my hand down the front of my pants so I could play with my clit. I rubbed eagerly, while I stroked him with my other hand and took him to the back of my throat again.

His nostrils flared and he sucked in a sharp breath as salty pre-come slid onto my tongue.

"You love the taste of your husband, don't you, little wife?" he said roughly.

Pleasure tightened his features, and the veins in his forearms popped when he curled his fingers into tight fists, fighting back his orgasm. I wanted to taste him on my tongue and feel him going down my throat. I wanted to make him moan, to make him fall apart for me. Tucker brought out a side of myself I never knew existed. He made me want things I never had before.

I sucked harder, stroked him faster, and he cursed loudly. "Oh no you don't," he said and slid his thumb into the corner of my mouth, stopping me. "This mouth's not getting my come, that perfect little pussy's gonna get it, wife."

Oh fuck. My inner muscles started clutching at nothing, and I rubbed my clit faster. He slid his cock from my mouth, and I whimpered as he reached down, hauled me off my feet, spun me around, and tossed me over the back of the couch.

He yanked down my tights and panties, and I barely had time to suck in a strangled breath before he slammed inside me. He was so fucking hard and thick and unrelenting. I jerked and cried out, my pussy gripping wildly around him, coming instantly.

"Fucking hell. Hungry little pussy can't get enough," he growled as he fucked into me so hard the heavy couch shuddered with every thrust.

My fingers dug into the cushions as my orgasm went on

and on, crying out for more with every brutal thrust. Finally, he slammed deep, grinding against my ass and pulsing heavily inside me. God, he filled me up, coming inside me hard and hot. All I could do was gasp, churning my hips as I shuddered, aftershocks of pleasure still rolling through me.

Tuck pulled out suddenly and flipped me over to my back, my hips were up on the arm of the couch, so my ass was up in the air, then he spread my pussy with his fingers, watching as he did it, and moaned again. "You're so full of my come, Libs. I want to fuck you so many times, it's dripping out of you." Then he lifted his gaze to me and, holding my stare, slid his fingers deep inside me.

I moaned, arching against the cushion. I was sensitive, but it felt really freaking good. He leaned over me, sliding a hand up my shirt, massaging one of my breasts as he eased his finger in and out of me. He started slow, increasing his speed until he was thrusting in and out of me fast. The wet sounds were obscene, and god, somehow that was so goddamn hot.

"Gonna finger-fuck my come deep inside you, darlin'. I want to feel this pussy coming again. You gonna come again for me, little wife?"

I couldn't catch my breath. I was twisting my hips, writhing. "Tucker," I gasped. "I'm...*oh fuck*." I came again, with a scream this time, my pussy trying to grip on to his thrusting fingers.

"Beautiful, Libs. So fucking beautiful when you come for me like that."

I collapsed back, panting, and Tuck slid his fingers from me carefully. I blinked up at him. I'd never experienced anything like that in my life. No other man had ever made me feel this good. My heart fluttered in my chest. This was so goddamn dangerous. He was dangerous.

"What are you thinking?" he asked low, his gaze moving over my face, a look in his eyes I couldn't read. "Tell me."

It was a soft demand, but it was a demand. He didn't want to know what the real Libby thought, he wanted to know what pretend Libby was thinking. Why did that hurt all of a sudden? Why did knowing he wanted me so badly that he'd created this version of us together—a fantasy—hurt so much?

Probably because I wanted this fantasy too? It was beautiful.

This was perfect.

"A few things," I said, my voice husky from the way he'd just made me scream, but mainly from the emotions he was making me feel, emotions I could not let myself feel.

"Yeah?" He leaned forward and tugged up my underwear and tights, then dragged me farther up the couch, and came down beside me. "Tell me."

His front was to my back, and he wrapped me in his big muscled arms, holding me to him. One of his wide palms rested on my belly, a part of my body I'd always been self-conscious of. I had rolls, cellulite, I was a bigger girl, but Tucker seemed to like my body the way it was, a lot.

I covered his hand with mine and shut down real Libby and gave him the fantasy version of me he truly wanted. "I was thinking my husband is so fucking hot and makes me come like I never have before," I said, though the latter of what I said was all true. "And that the way you fuck me, the way you make love to me...it won't be long before you get me pregnant."

His rough exhale tickled my neck, and he tightened his hold on me. I could feel his heart beating hard against my back as silence stretched out between us. "You're the best thing that's ever happened to me, Libs," he finally said. "I need you to know that, baby."

He tugged my tights down again and slid back inside me, fucking me again, slow and deep this time. His arms stayed around me and his big body shuddered when we finally came together a short time later.

He pressed a kiss to the side of my throat, and I lay there cocooned in his strong arms. The sounds of his breathing as it evened out and the crackle of the fire, along with the heat of his body soaking through me, had my eyes growing heavy. I tried to fight it, but I was so comfy. Tucker had worn me out.

So I let my eyes slide closed, warm and safe in his arms.

Chapter Six

Tucker

RUTH JUMPED up on the tractor beside me, again like she'd done it before.

"So how many cows do you have?" she asked as I started the engine and headed across the field.

"Enough that I won't go hungry, but not so many that it takes up all my time."

She grinned at me. "Sounds sensible."

"I can be sensible," I said, glancing at her gorgeous mouth. Yesterday I'd promised to show her around—hard to do that when we were playing, because my wife would already know everything about the property—so no black clothes this morning. Although I'd come prepared.

So far I'd taken her out to meet the chickens and let them out of their coop, though a few of the less brave ones had stepped out, seen the light dusting of snow, and headed straight back inside.

I glanced at Ruth again, and my lips twitched. She was fucking adorable in one of my woolen hats. It was too big for her and so were the mittens I'd dug out. They'd been mine when I was a kid, but they were still too big for those petite little hands of hers.

"So what do you do to make a buck?" she asked. "Or are you one of those reclusive millionaires who abandons the real world and hides away in a remote location?"

I chuckled. "Not a millionaire, sadly. I do a lot of carpentry. I make things and sell them to stores in the city."

"What kind of things?"

"I can show you my workshop when we get back if you like?"

Her smile widened. "I'd love that."

I stopped at the gate, and before I could open my door, Ruth had jumped down and run over to open the gate. She stood waiting for me to drive through, shut it after us, then climbed back up. The cows followed as I drove out to the middle of the field. I expected Ruth to be scared, cows were large animals, but she got down when I did, climbed onto the trailer with me, and as soon as I cut through the baling twine, she grabbed a few slices of hay and tossed it out, helping me like a pro.

"You've done this before," I said.

Her head spun to me, and there was a cute-as-fuck blush to her cheeks. "Well, yeah, I grew up on a farm."

My brows shot up. "You did? Where?"

She bit her lip and glanced away, grabbing more hay. "Colorado."

"Really?" That was seriously weird.

"Yep."

I'm not sure why I was surprised, probably because Ruth's story was so similar to Libby's. Libs had lived on a farm in Colorado, before she'd run off to California. Both women had left farms to pursue acting careers, but then I guess that was the same story for a lot of folks. Leaving a small town or whatever and heading to the city to try to make it big. "Damn," I said. "I could've had you out here working sooner."

Her laugher sent tingles dancing over my scalp and across my shoulders. I fucking loved this woman's laugh. It was sweet, musical, something else she had in common with my Libby. I'd worked so hard to get her to laugh during our weekly radio calls. I'd wanted to make her happy, and yeah, I'd wanted to feel those tingles I thought only she could give me. Apparently, I was wrong.

By the time we finished feeding the animals and I showed her a few of my favorite spots around the property, it was late afternoon. I parked the tractor and Ruth jumped down. I glanced at my bag where my black beanie was tucked inside. The plan was to switch it out sometime during the day, but I was enjoying getting to know Ruth.

Jumping down from the tractor as well, I took her hand and led her into my workshop. The scent of cedar washed over us when we walked in. I flicked on the lights, and they blinked above us several times before lighting up the large space. In the middle of the room was a huge table where my finished items were being prepared to send out. The amount of orders I'd been getting was the reason I had Ruth here for only two weeks and not a month, something I was already regretting. The first load of finished pieces would go with Cash at the end of Ruth's stay, when he flew in to pick her up.

I watched as she took in the workshop, raised her eyes to the mezzanine above us, then rushed to the table, picking up one of my cedar bowls. She spun back to me, brows raised. "This is...this is stunning, Tuck."

Each one was unique, designed around the individual piece of wood, following its own distinct shape, accentuating its knots and dips and ridges. It was a labor of love, and I charged well for the time I put into each peace. "Thanks, baby," I said, the endearment slipping out easily.

She didn't seem to mind or even notice as she walked around the table checking everything out. Honestly, it was starting to get hard to separate Ruth from the character she played for me.

When she looked up again, her eyes were bright and filled with joy. "You love this...doing this, don't you?"

All I could do was fucking nod, unable to take my eyes off her. The sincerity of the emotion in her gaze, of how moved she was by my work—knowing how much I loved it and what it meant to me—was a fucking punch in the chest.

She nodded, running her fingers over different pieces. "I can see it. God, I can feel it in every piece on this table." She looked up again. "I'm so happy for you, Tuck, that you have this. Not everyone understands what it's like to create something they love, something that they're proud of. You did that."

Jesus, my fucking throat felt tight. "You do," I said. "With your writing, and when you're acting."

Her smile widened, but it didn't seem to reach her eyes. "Yeah," she said. "Exactly." She motioned across the room. "So what's up the stairs?"

"A guest room. Cash and Riley use it when they come and stay." There was a look in her eyes I couldn't read, and I wanted to know what was going on in her head right now. I had no right to push for more from this woman, she didn't owe me more than she was already giving me, but I couldn't stop myself. "Talk to me. Tell me what you're thinking."

She laughed softly, trying to make light, to pretend I hadn't seen what I had in her eyes. "Oh nothing, ignore me." She motioned to the table. "Just...not all of us are as talented as you, Mr. Smith. I've had a script with my agent for close to a year, and no one's biting."

"They will," I said.

She laughed again. "You're sweet."

"Not being sweet, Ruth. Okay, sure, I've only known you a handful of days, but I just...I know I'm right."

"See, totally sweet."

I winked. "What's the play about?"

She stilled, blinking up at me. "Lost love."

Her voice had grown husky. "Yeah?"

She nodded.

"You writing from experience?" I asked, because I had to fucking know.

"I am," she said, her gaze sliding from mine.

Why the hell did I feel, shit, jealous, of whoever this asshole was who had loved Ruth, then let her slip away? "Sorry to hear that, darlin', but that's why it'll be too good to pass up. I know it's only a matter of time before you sell it."

Her eyes sparkled. "Thanks, but now I'm going to blame you for jinxing me if nothing comes of it."

I grinned. "If anything, I'm manifesting it for you. The universe will have to listen now."

"You're very charming," she said out of the blue. "But I think you know that."

I knew no such thing. Still, I winked. "I try."

She closed the short distance between us and looked up at me. "I'm glad I came here and that I'm getting to spend time with you."

There was nothing but sincerity in her pretty eyes.

Fuck, I liked this girl.

Tucking her hair behind her ear, I slid my hand down the side of her lovely face and held her chin. "I'm glad you're here too, darlin'." Then I went with it, this moment that was genuine, and real, and leaned in and kissed her.

I'd kissed her quite a few times now, but only when we were playing. This was the first time I'd kissed Ruth, and she was just as eager now as she'd been the other times. She pressed her curvy little body more tightly against me and wrapped her arms around my waist. Gently squeezing her soft hip, I pulled her closer and slid my other hand into her hair, kissing her deeper.

When I finally lifted my head, I smiled down at her, trying to keep things light for now. It wasn't easy when all I could think about was bending her over my workbench and fucking her. As much as I wanted to do that—and I got the feeling Ruth would be down for that as well, going by her shaky breaths and the hot look in her eyes—it would have to wait. We'd been out most of the day, taking longer than I'd expected. "I need to feed you before I fuck you again," I said and gave her another soft kiss.

"I'm fine. Honestly, I'm happy to wait—" Her stomach rumbled, *loudly*.

Her cheeks went up in flames, and I had to bite back my moan. Fuck, I *loved* those blushes. "What were you saying?"

"Fine, you win."

Chuckling, I took her hand, led her outside, and across to the house.

Ruth helped me make a quick supper. Nothing fancy, just some steaks and eggs.

"You wanna eat in the living room tonight?"

"Sounds good." The fire was lit and it was warm and cozy.

Ruth carried our plates to the couch, and I poured us both a drink.

"What's this?" Ruth asked, studying her glass.

"Apple pie moonshine."

"Moonshine? I've never had it before."

"Make sure you just sip it. It's potent."

She took a tentative sip and coughed. "Oh wow, you're not wrong." She tilted her head to the side and her brows lifted. "It has a really nice aftertaste though. I get the apples now."

"It's a Smith family recipe."

She took another sip and her cheeks turned pink again, but this time I'd guess it was from the moonshine. "I like it." She put her glass aside. "So do you have family in the area?"

I chewed my steak and nodded. "There are Smiths scattered all over these mountains, but I see Beau, Hank, and Cash more than the others. They live farther down the mountain with their wives and kids, and Cash, who you've met, his wife, Riley, is actually a writer as well."

She perked up. "Really?"

I nodded and took another sip of my drink. "She's a romance author."

Her brows shot up. "I'm a huge romance reader. What name does she write under?"

"Her maiden name, Riley Lewis."

Her eyes widened. "Oh my god! I love her books. I've read all of them." She blinked over at me, looking stunned. "I was in a plane with Riley Lewis's husband and I never even knew it." She shook her head. "I mean, it's obvious now that you've told me. She dedicates every book to Cash. Wow, that's so cool."

I couldn't contain my smile. Seeing her this excited was infectious. "I have most of them as well." I motioned to my bookshelf with my fork. "If you want, I could get Cash to bring you a signed copy of one of her books when he comes back?"

"Could you really?"

I nodded and winked. "No trouble. Riley loves me."

She chuckled. "I don't doubt it. That would be amazing. Thank you."

I shrugged. "Nothing to it."

She laughed then, full and throaty and sexy as hell. "You're just showing off now."

"Maybe," I said and grabbed the mason jar I'd brought in with me and held it up.

She nodded, all pink cheeked and eyes bright with happiness and held out her glass for more.

"So what kind of farm did you grow up on?"

Ruth stilled, her shoulders kind of coming up. "We had cattle mainly."

"Farm life wasn't for you?"

She sipped her drink. "Nope. I thought it was because I hated the solitude, but..."

When she said no more, I gave her a little nudge. "But?"

She shrugged. "I'm starting to think it was more about the people I was stuck with."

Maybe I was heading into territory she didn't want me to go, but I had to ask. "You don't get on with your parents?"

"More like they didn't get on with each other...or more, my father was an abusive asshole and there was no escape." Her gaze shot to me, alarm covering her face. "Sorry, I didn't mean to say that...that wasn't something I planned to dump on you." She shook her head and chuckled awkwardly. "It's this moonshine."

Everything in me had frozen; every muscle in my body going rock solid. "Your father was abusive?"

Her gaze was darting around the room, as if she was looking for an escape.

"Ruth, we don't have to—"

"This just got really heavy, really quickly. God, you're probably thinking all kinds of things." She shook her head again. "I mean, yes, he was abusive. He liked to hit, mainly my mother, occasionally me, but it sounds worse than it was. Sorry, I don't know why I shared that. Can we just drop it now?"

My hand beside me had curled into a fist. All I could envision was slamming it into her weak, fucking bastard father's face. I stretched my fingers out, shoving down my anger, and nodded. "Yeah, of course. I'm sorry, Ruth."

"No, it's fine, I'm fine. Really."

I changed the subject, got us some ice cream for dessert, then I spent the next hour trying to make her laugh by telling her stories about me, Hank, Beau, and Cash when we were kids, the things we got up to when our families got together. Every time she let loose that musical laugh, it felt like a win.

Ruth was tipsy from the moonshine and, thankfully, a lot more relaxed. She scooped up her last mouthful of dessert, then glanced at me and snort-giggled. I looked down to where she was looking and I realized I'd spilled melted ice cream down the front of my shirt.

"Jesus," I said, putting down my bowl, then I tugged off my shirt and grabbed a fresh one from the clean laundry basket sitting on the window seat and dropped back down beside her.

I glanced at Ruth and she blinked, then something shifted in her eyes, and she put down her empty bowl and crawled over to me, pressing into my side.

"Hey," I said, grinning down at her. It was as if she'd read my mind. I'd wanted her closer all fucking night.

She slid her hand up my chest. "I've been doing some research," she said, "you wanna hear what I've learned, honey?"

Her voice was a little different, so was the way she was looking at me. My gaze dropped to her hand on my chest, and I realized I'd put on a black shirt without even thinking about it. She'd jumped straight into character. No more Ruth looking up at me with that needy expression, this was Libby. She was fucking hot, sexy, and having her draped over me like this, just her hand on my chest, had me hard for her, but a part of me wished she was still Ruth, that we weren't playing.

But then she sat up and tugged off her shirt, tossing it on the floor, and before I had a chance to register that, she reached back and unhooked her bra, tossing that aside as well.

"Fuck, darlin'." I choked, eating up the sight of her.

She ran her hands over those full breasts, cupping them, toying with her nipples. "When you get me pregnant, these" —she massaged the soft mounds and my breath caught in my throat—"they'll get bigger, and my nipples will darken." She took one of my hands and placed it on her breast to cup her.

I took over, pushing her hands away and using both of mine. "Yeah, tell me what else," I choked out, pulled into the scene with her.

She licked her lips. "Because of the increased blood flow, my pussy might change. It could look a little swollen, like we've spent a long night fucking. It'll be more sensitive as well." She straddled me and ground against my hard cock while I played with her tits. "And I'm gonna be so horny,

Tuck. Some pregnant women are insatiable. I'm gonna need my husband to fuck me all the time."

Fucking hell, I was panting now, and with that, I was lost, I was right there with her, in a little bubble of make-believe. "While you were away, I stroked myself to thoughts of holding you down and filling you with my come. Of breeding this tight little body over and over again."

She trembled against me. "I did too."

I'd wanted inside this woman all day, and I snapped. Tossing her onto the couch I came down on top of her, relishing the soft curves of her breasts and belly, then taking her wrists, I held them over her head. "You did this to me, Libby, it's all your fault. This curvy little body was made to be fucked, to be bred. Now I'm going to pump you full of come and you're going to hold it there inside you, understand me?"

She nodded, gasping as I held her wrists with my hand and yanked down her pants and underwear with the other. She pulled one leg free of the fabric and wrapped both of her legs around me, while I shakily undid my belt and jeans, freeing my cock.

I didn't wait. I stared down at her, our eyes locked as I pushed inside her, stuffing her full with one smooth stroke. "You exist to take my cock, Libs, to get pregnant by me," I growled, the words coming from a part of me I didn't know existed, as I began fucking her frantically, like I believed the shit I'd just said, like my life depended on filling her up, on breeding my curvy little wife.

She arched against me. "*Oh god.*" Her nails dug into my skin as she clung to me. "Do you have any idea how good you feel inside me without a condom?" She groaned against my ear. "I love it when you come inside me. Please, I need you to come inside me."

I shuddered and rocked into her harder, faster, then lifted my head and looked down at her. "Because you're mine, aren't you, Libby? You're mine, and once I've put a baby inside you, you won't go anywhere. You'll never leave me, will you, darlin'?"

She shook her head. "I'll never leave, never again."

Then she moaned loudly, and I felt her pussy clutch around me so fucking tight before she came, crying out, gripping rhythmically around my cock and pulling me along with her.

I fucked into her, pounding her like a goddamn barbarian, then I was coming deep inside her, grinding and groaning. "Fucking take it, Libby, take it all and don't you dare lose one drop."

She nodded, eyes half lidded, panting, while her legs were locked around me, holding me inside her, making sure she gave me what I asked for.

I lowered my weight, still deep inside her, rocking more gently now, and buried my face in her hair while I tried to catch my breath, but it was hard, because I was fucking shaken.

What the fuck had just come over me? Where the fuck had I gone? I'd been so deep in the scene, I hadn't seen Ruth beneath me, I'd seen Libby, only Libby, and I didn't know how to deal with the feelings slamming into me one after another.

So I stayed where I was, and when my cock softened and I slipped out of her, I rolled to my side and held her against me, fucking hiding just how much I was feeling.

Because I realized now, just how much losing Libby had truly broken me.

Chapter Seven

Libby

SOMEHOW, a week had already passed. Seven days of the best orgasms of my life, hanging with Tucker, my best friend, only he had no idea it was the real Libby sleeping beside him every night.

Chewing my lip, I glanced out the window. It was the first time I'd been on my own since I got here. It was lightly snowing, and Tuck was out there somewhere chopping down trees for firewood. It looked like he had more than enough wood to me, but it had seemed pretty important to him when he'd left a couple hours ago. So I guess I was wrong.

I'd decided to use the alone time to work, and my laptop was open on the table. I hadn't had a chance to check my email that often since I got here, and when I checked earlier, there was a message from my agent. Someone was interested in my script. I needed to do some edits, then send it back ASAP. This was exciting...beyond exciting. I'd had interest before, only to have it sputter out, so I was trying not to get my hopes up, but this felt different.

The fact that I was here with Tucker when I heard

news about this particular script wasn't lost on me. This wasn't just any story, this was *our* story. I'd started writing it as a way of dealing with the loss I felt without him in my life. It had consumed me, was my best work, and the script that had finally landed me an agent.

When he'd asked me what my play was about, I thought I'd freaking perish right there and then. Rubbing at the goose bumps that now prickled across my arms, I ignored the swirl of nerves and guilt inside me and forced myself to read over the scene I'd rewritten. I made a few notes, then got back to editing.

I looked up when I heard the door close, followed by the thud of boots on the kitchen floor. I'd been so focused that hours had passed, and I suddenly realized I was sitting in the dark.

Tucker switched on the light, shrugging off his puffer jacket. His face was flushed from the cold, and his gaze moved over me, then the laptop and the stack of notes beside me.

"What's going on?" His gorgeous lips curled up as he tugged off his woolen hat.

Before I knew what I was doing, I'd shot to my feet, rounded the table, and ran at him. I wrapped my arms around him, my excitement bubbling inside me. "I got an email from my agent. There's serious interest in my script!"

His smile widened. "Fuck, baby, that's awesome. What did I say?"

I chuckled. "Yes, yes, you are the all-seeing oracle." I didn't know if we were in character or not. Honestly, we had kind of fallen into this in-between. Or maybe it was that even when we weren't in character, we were affectionate, and yeah, couldn't keep our hands off each other. I wanted him constantly, and I wasn't going to waste one minute of my limited time with him.

"That's right," he said, his eyes lighting up before flexing his biceps. "Glad you're finally seeing it."

God, Tucker had me in a constant state of wanting to swoon, laugh, and jump him in unison. "I just have to do some edits and send it back...but, I can do it later. I don't want to cut into your—"

"Fuck that," he said, not letting me finish. "You do what you have to do, and I'll make dinner."

We never brought up the reason I was here, and Tucker obviously didn't want me to either. "You've been out working all day. You shouldn't have to do that. I'll finish this, then cook for you. I'm not even hungry," I lied.

"When was the last time you ate?"

I bit my lip.

"You haven't eaten since breakfast, have you?"

I shook my head.

He took my chin, kissed me hard, then slapped me on the ass. "Get back to work, woman. Let your man cook for you."

I nodded and wondered what he saw in my eyes when I looked up at him. Could he see the truth? I thought I couldn't love him more before we were thrown together like this, but I'd been wrong—I was so gone for this man, it was terrifying. I'd tried really freaking hard not to let myself fall for him, but I had. It was impossible not to.

"Thanks," I whispered, then lifted on my toes and took another kiss, this one soft and sweet.

He smiled against my lips. "Anything for you, Libs," he said huskily. Then stepped back and tugged off his sweater, revealing a black thermal.

Okay, so we were in play.

I went back to the table, and it was hard to look away from him and get back to work as he moved around the kitchen, but I forced myself to do it. This was my future, this script, my life back in the city. Even if I had changed my mind, even if I never wanted to leave here, I couldn't stay, because Tucker would never forgive me for this deception. He'd be humiliated, angry, hurt. The time to own up was the minute I walked off that plane and recognized him.

I'd chosen not to. I chose to live out my own fantasy.

Any way you looked at it, what I'd done was totally messed up.

Shoving those thoughts from my mind, I ignored the guilt and regret and got back to work.

❄

Tucker

Slinging the towel around my hips, I stepped out of the shower. After dinner, I'd left Libby...fuck, Ruth, working on her script. She'd been so excited. The way she'd lit up when she told me her news was branded on my fucking brain. Quickly drying off, I rubbed the towel over my hair. Shit was getting fucking complicated.

After I'd put on that black shirt without thinking several days ago, and we'd fucked on the couch—the way she'd pulled me into that scene, the way I'd reacted to the things she'd said—something had changed. The lines were blurred somehow. Reality and fantasy were mingling, and I was starting to have trouble separating the two.

I wanted this woman twenty-four seven, which was why I'd forced myself to leave the house today. I'd fucked her multiple times a day since she'd gotten here. She seemed to want it, but then she was paid to make me think that, right? And I was getting—who the fuck was I kidding, I already *was* addicted to her, and not just when she was playing Libby. It had all become too goddamn intense. My head was all over the place. Honestly, the woman downstairs had me fucking mesmerized, and when she played Libby, it was too real, or at least how I'd always imagined things with Libs would be if she were here with me.

So yeah, I'd left this morning, even though I already had more than enough wood to last the winter and halfway through the next, because I was feeling things for this girl that I shouldn't. There was something almost...familiar about her, even when she was out of character. She made me feel like I could totally be myself, and I was terrified that when she left in a week's time, I wouldn't fucking recover from it.

I shoved my fingers through my hair. I needed to get this thing back on track. I had to stop thinking like this and remember why she was here. Ruth was being paid to fuck me. She was an escort, and an actor, and that look in her eyes that made my heart pound and my fucking palms sweat was just an act as well, all part of the role she was playing. She wasn't falling for me, there would be no happily ever after for us—because she wasn't Libby.

Ruth was here for me, to make all my dirty fucking dreams and deepest fantasies come true.

It didn't matter how I'd feel after she left. I'd worry about that when it happened. For now, while I had her here, I was going to make the most of it.

Tossing my towel in the laundry basket, I strode into my

room and tugged on a pair of black track pants. I'd had a bit of a wobble the last few days, that's all, but I was solid now. I was good, and I wanted to play.

The fire was roaring downstairs, so I didn't bother with a shirt, and by the time I jogged downstairs and hit the living room, I was back in the fantasy and hard as fuck for my little wife.

Being away from her all day, after fucking her so often, had been torture, but then it had been totally self-inflicted. I'd wasted precious time.

When I walked into the living room, I almost fell over my own fucking feet. She was sitting cross-legged in front of the fire, her reading glasses, which I'd seen for the first time today when I walked into the kitchen, still perched on her nose while she flicked through one of the books from my shelf. Christ, her lips were darker, puffy from her biting them while she'd been focused on her work.

She glanced up and smiled at me, then her gaze immediately slid down my bare chest and landed on my dick that was tenting the front of my track pants, and her lips parted.

I said nothing as I strode across the living room and sat in my recliner.

"You've been working hard all day. Feel better after a nice shower?" she asked, turning to fully face me.

"Would've been better if you'd joined me." My voice sounded deeper, rougher from how much I wanted her, and I didn't even try to hide it, there was no reason to.

"All you had to do was ask and I would've come and scrubbed your back," she said, that cute, sexy smile curving her pretty lips.

I rested a hand on my stomach, and her gaze was drawn to the movement. I slid my palm up and down my abs. She didn't move, watching, waiting. She may be doing this for the money, but there was no missing the way she was breathing faster or the little tremor that moved through her sweet, curvy body.

Hooking my hand in the waistband of my pants, I pushed them down and my cock sprung free. I hooked the elastic under my balls, and my little wife sucked in a breath. My cock was like a hot steel rod against my stomach. Fuck, I ached for some attention from this woman.

I crooked my finger at her. "Come here, Libby, it's about time you looked after your husband."

She didn't stand. She shifted onto her hands and knees, then fucking crawled toward me. Seeing her like that, the hungry look on her face... Yeah, fuck, new kink unlocked. I'd never been overly dominant. I liked to laugh, have fun, but there was something about this girl, or maybe this situation, that was bringing out a different side of me.

You know exactly what is doing this to you.

My Libby, the real Libby, had fucking broken me. She'd broken my heart when she'd left me all alone. I'd lived for our once-a-week radio calls when we were kids, and I'd checked my email constantly when she'd gone off to college and we continued to talk as we'd gotten older. I'd wanted more, and I'd pushed for it. I'd made sure she understood where I wanted our relationship to go, but I'd pushed hard —too fucking hard, because she'd cut me off as if I'd never existed. All my fantasies of one day flying to visit her, or her coming here to see me, of finally holding her for real, of kissing her, making love to her had been blown apart. I'd only seen one photo of her, the one she'd sent me. I hadn't even been able to see her face clearly, but I didn't need to know what she looked like, that didn't matter to me because I was already in love with her.

I'd dreamed of getting down on one knee, of asking her

to marry me. I'd seen our wedding, played out the honeymoon in my head, then imagined her growing round with our babies. Our lives together had become real to me. I'd believed in it, that one day I'd have that with her.

Yeah, it was messed up, naive maybe, but every part of me had believed it.

I was hurt, and I was fucking angry.

Hurting her back wasn't something I wanted, but I did want to punish her, I realized. I wanted to show her what she'd missed out on. Right then, I wanted to take her over my knee and spank her until she begged for my forgiveness for breaking me, for breaking us. I wanted her to shake and cry while she came for me—I wanted her to tell me how much she loved me. How much she would always love me, just as I would her.

I spread my legs wider so my dream girl could crawl between them.

That's the real reason this sexy little woman kneeling between my knees, gripping my thighs and waiting for my next order, was here. Not just to live out the sweet part of my fantasy, the fucking and laughing, the affection and companionship, but because I needed to hear her tell me she was sorry as well, for throwing me away. I hadn't realized it until now, or how badly I needed to hear her apologize, but I did. Before I let my Libby go for real, I needed to hear it, and this was the only way I could.

I kept my hands on the arms of the chair. "You went away," I said roughly, the words wrenched from me. "You left me here all alone, and you didn't say goodbye."

My little wife stilled, then blinked up at me, it was just for a split second, before she drew in a shaky breath. I could see the wheels turning behind those beautiful eyes, switching gears, following my lead. Finally, she licked her lips, biting down on the side of the lower one. It made her look innocent and sexy, and made me even fucking harder. Her hands on my thighs flexed, squeezing. "I...I'm so sorry, Tuck," she choked out.

I shook my head. "That's not enough, it's nowhere near good enough," I said, shaking, almost fucking panting at this point. This wasn't me, I wasn't this man, or at least I hadn't thought I was. But fuck, I needed this. "You're going to have to show me how sorry you are."

Her lashes fluttered. Christ, her eyes were actually glossy as she swallowed audibly. "Whatever you need to believe me, to believe just how sorry I am, I'll do it."

I believed her. I believed everything out of her perfect, pouty mouth. I gripped the arms of my chair harder. "You can start by sucking my cock down your pretty throat, as deep as you can get it." I held her gaze. "I want to hear you choking on it, Libby, do you understand?"

Her cheeks darkened even more, but she nodded. "I understand."

Chapter Eight

Libby

My heart was pounding wildly. Every word he'd just said was for *me,* for his Libby. I'd hurt him. I'd gone away. I'd left him alone and I hadn't said goodbye. I'd made him feel that way—so hurt. Unwanted. Abandoned.

"I'm sorry," I choked out again as I took his long, hard length in my hand and shuffled closer on my knees.

"I don't want useless words, Libby, you need to *show* me."

This was a different Tucker. He was hurt, angry. When we were able to talk over the phone, and in his emails, his tone was always light and sweet, fun. The pain I'd caused him was there in his eyes now, and in his voice. He wasn't acting, this wasn't him role-playing, not really, he was using me to release all that pain, to get the closure he'd needed from me four years ago but had never received.

Nodding, I sucked his cock into my mouth, taking him as deep as I could. I wanted to show him how sorry I was. Right then, it was everything. The broad head bumped the back of my throat and I choked a little. His fingers wound in my hair, fisting it firmly so he could use it to set the pace, not shoving me down on him, but letting me know he was in control.

I realized Tucker needed it, he needed that control over me because I'd made him feel powerless. He was up here in the mountains, and when I stopped replying, he had no way of talking to me, of finding me. His hips lifted a little when I sucked him back down and I gagged. Tears welled in my eyes, running down my cheeks as I did it again and again, desperate to give him what he needed, to make him forgive me for the way I'd hurt him.

Pre-come slid from the tip of his cock, and I lapped it up, running my tongue down his length, then I opened my throat and swallowed, clutching the head of his cock.

Tucker groaned, then pulsed in my mouth, coming down my throat without warning. Gripping a hard thigh with one hand, I did my best to swallow it all.

My throat was still working around him when he tapped my jaw and eased me away from his cock, then he was hauling me up into his lap and pressing his mouth to my ear. "That was a good start, Libs, but you're not nearly sorry enough yet."

I nodded. Whatever he needed, I'd give it to him. I'd do this all night if that's what he needed from me.

"I think you need to be spanked," he said roughly.

I sucked in a sharp breath, and Tucker stilled, waiting for what I was going to do or say. All I had to say was no, and he'd stop. I knew that with everything in me. I didn't want to say it, though. I wouldn't.

"Yes," I rasped. "Please, I need you to spank me. I need you to know how sorry I am."

He hissed through his teeth, then he tossed me over his lap.

Oh god. I'd never done anything like this, and I couldn't

help but squirm. I was a mix of apprehension and anticipation.

"Ready?" he said roughly.

"Yes—"

Tucker's hand came down on my ass over my tights.

A startled cry left me, and I jerked and squirmed on his lap as the sting radiated from the point of contact.

"Keep still," he said, "and take what your husband gives you. You know it's what you deserve."

I bit my lip and nodded.

His hand slid over my spandex-clad ass, squeezing one cheek, then the other, and I was all but panting to keep myself from squirming again.

He tugged my tights and underwear down, exposing my bare ass. Tucker growled low, like a freaking grizzly, and gripped one of my ass cheeks again, but tighter. "I told you, you needed to be a good girl, Libby. I told you, but you weren't, were you?"

I shook my head, more tears welling in my eyes. "N-no."

"No," he repeated. "You were very bad."

"I'm sorry," I choked out.

He made another rough sound. "You treated me like I was nothing, like I was nothing to you...when you were everything to me."

I swallowed down my sob, his words like blows to my heart, coming one after another.

His hand came down on my ass then, before I could beg his forgiveness, and I jolted again, a cry bursting from me.

He rested his hand where he'd spanked me, massaging over my hot, stinging flesh. "Tell me you're sorry again."

"I-I'm sorry."

His hand came down again, on the other cheek this time. "I don't believe you. Again."

"I'm s-sorry, Tucker. I'm so sorry."

Another slap, this one harder. I hung on to the arm of the chair, moaning into the fabric. It stung, but it...god, it sent throbbing heat to my core.

"Again."

"I'm sorry," I cried out, louder this time.

Slap. "Again."

My pussy clutched, spasming around nothing. I moaned louder. "I'm sorry," I sobbed, this time unable to hold back my cry, and I squirmed because I couldn't stop myself. My thighs were slick, sliding against each other.

Slap. "Tell me you'll never leave me again," he said, breathing heavily, his big frame trembling under me.

I squeezed my eyes closed, my ass lifting higher as I jolted against him. "I'll never leave you again," I choked out.

His hot palm slid over my throbbing cheek and he massaged it, then dipped his fingers between my tightly clenched thighs, sliding over my pussy, teasing the opening, dipping the tip of his finger inside me.

"Tucker, please."

He was breathing heavily, the silence stretching out.

"Tell me you love me," he finally said, his big body shaking now as he slid two fingers deep inside me, making me gasp.

I whimpered, my heart slamming wildly in my chest. I did. I did love him, but I couldn't say it. I couldn't say the words, because there would be no taking them back. He wouldn't know they were real, but I'd know, and if I said them, how could I leave him? How could I leave him alone again?

I tried to spread wider for him, but my tights and underwear just above my knees stopped me. "Please," I gasped out again.

He yanked his fingers from me and slapped my pussy. I cried out and squeezed my thighs together as tightly as I could, moaning when I almost came.

"Say it," he said, his voice rough, broken. "I need to hear you say it, Libby. Tell me you love me."

More tears slid down my cheeks. I was close to falling apart. My emotions were all over the place, my heart was breaking, while it pumped full at the same time. He loved me, but I could never have him, not now, not after this. Not after hurting him the way I had, then coming here and lying to him, keeping the truth from him.

"Say it," he said again, louder, a demand.

He needed it, he needed that from me, I heard it in the desperation in his voice.

He brought his hand down on my ass one more time. "I love you," I cried out, jolting against him, the words forced from deep within me.

He released a ragged breath and lifted me, planting me on the floor on my hands and knees, then Tucker was behind me, the head of his cock pressed against my opening.

"Say it again," he rasped.

I dragged in a shudder, biting back another sob. "I love you."

He slammed inside me, and I came instantly, screaming his name. Tucker didn't slow, he fucked me so hard my arms gave out.

"My precious little wife, my perfect Libby," he said roughly. "I love you. I fucking love you." He groaned as he thrust into me over and over, deep and hard, claiming me in a way I didn't know was possible, in a way I felt branded from it—that I would never recover from.

He didn't slow, didn't let up, and I came again with a desperate moan, spasming around his relentless cock.

"That's it, that's it, darlin'," he groaned. "Take it, take it all. Gonna put a baby in that soft belly, then you won't leave, then you won't ever leave me."

I whimpered. "Please, I need to feel you coming inside me."

Tucker growled and cursed, then slammed in so deep, he forced the air from my lungs. His cock throbbed heavily, filling me, and he didn't stop his brutal thrusts until he was completely spent.

I lay beneath him, gasping, trying to catch my breath, my mind spinning and my body humming. My ass was hot and tingling, and my pussy was sensitive and still lightly pulsing.

Tucker ran his hand down my back and over my bottom, then he cursed. "Are you okay?" he choked out. "Ruth? Shit, are you all right?"

He'd scared himself. I heard it in his voice. "I'm good," I said as he wrapped his arms around me and lifted me off the floor. "I promise," I said and watched as his eyes widened on my face.

I knew without looking that my mouth was dark and puffy from biting my lips when he spanked me, and I could only guess that my eyes were red and puffy like the rest of my face from crying.

"I made you cry," he said, sounding horrified. "Fuck, what you told me about your father...what he did...I didn't mean to—"

I pressed my fingers to his lips. "Yes, I cried, but not because you hurt me." Not physically, anyway. The truth hurts, and Tuck had hammered home the truth of what I'd done. "The scene, it was intense, that's all."

"I hit you. Your ass is red, my handprint—"

I stopped him again. "I liked being spanked, and I liked

the way you took me, don't you dare think otherwise. I consented because I wanted it too. I think"—I looked into his haunted eyes—"that what we just did was somehow healing for you."

His Adam's apple slid up and down his throat and he nodded.

I gave him a soft smile and held the side of his face, my palm against his beard, and slid my thumb over the smooth skin of his cheek above it. "Well, it was for me as well."

"It was?" he asked roughly, hopefully.

"I think I needed that as much as you did." He had no idea how much.

He released a shuddering breath, then slid his fingers into my hair, drawing me closer and kissed my forehead. Then he looked down at me. "Now I'm gonna take care of you," he said, lifting me in his arms and heading upstairs.

He set me on the bed and strode into the bathroom. I heard the water turn on. He was filling the tub. Tuck came back out and helped me out of my clothes, because I was still feeling shaky after what we'd just done. His gaze moved over my naked body. There was concern, tenderness, and somehow there was hunger still in his eyes as well.

I watched as he stripped, then he scooped me back up.

"I can walk, you know," I said, laughing a little.

He strode into the bathroom and pressed a soft kiss to my lips. "My woman doesn't walk when I can carry her."

His woman. We were back to playing, obviously. I pressed a kiss to his chest, and he squeezed me tighter, then stepped into the bath, maneuvering me so I was between his legs, my back to his front.

"Comfortable?" he asked, running his hands up and down my arms.

"Extremely. I could stay right here all night."

Then I sat there as he slowly, carefully washed my hair, then ran a soft washcloth over my body. He didn't call me Libby or Ruth the whole time, but he made me feel special.

By the time he was done, my eyes were stinging and there were more tears threatening.

Tucker could have been mine.

But I'd been a coward. And I'd thrown him away.

Chapter Nine

Libby

Tucker didn't wear black the next day, or the two days after that. He'd been affectionate, kind, sweet to me, he'd kissed me, hugged me, but he hadn't tried to take it further.

My sweet mountain man was struggling with everything he was feeling. I could see it, but my time with him had almost run out. The day after tomorrow, I would be leaving him. These were my last days, my last two nights with Tucker Smith.

It was as if he'd vanquished me completely, the idea of me anyway, the last time we role-played, and he didn't want to risk going back there. He still liked Ruth, but he'd performed an exorcism on Libby, and he didn't want her... *me*...back.

I wasn't sure what to do. I glanced out the window to the workshop. He'd gone out there this morning to finish the last few orders, bowls that would be going in the plane with me to the city.

My stomach churned at the thought of saying goodbye. I wasn't ready for this to end.

Grabbing the sandwich I'd made him, and the mug of

coffee, I headed out to his workshop. Music was playing quietly when I walked in. Tucker stood on one side of the room, utterly focused on what he was working on.

There was a small potbelly stove in the corner, and the room was lovely and warm. The smell of the wood he worked with filled the space, and I knew for the rest of my life, the smell of cedar would bring me back here, to this time, to Tucker.

He'd taken off his jacket, wearing only a T-shirt, and his strong forearms and sculpted biceps bunched and flexed as he worked, as he ran those wide palms over the smooth wood, caressing every surface with those long, thick fingers. Tucker Smith was beautiful all the time, but like this, he was utterly captivating.

I'd been standing there staring, so I cleared my throat.

His head jerked my way and his eyes lit up. "Hey, didn't see you there."

"You were pretty focused," I said, making my way over to him. "I made you some lunch. Thought you might've lost track of time."

He brushed his hands off on his jeans and gave me one of his gorgeous smiles. "I did, yeah." He took the sandwich and mug. "Thanks, darlin', this looks great." He lifted his plate. "Where's yours?"

When Tuck was here on his own, hours passing while he worked, losing track of time, there was no one to look after him, no one to bring him a sandwich or a coffee when he'd been working all day. I hated the thought of it. "I'm fine. I'm still full after the breakfast you made." I motioned to the tatty old couch against the wall. "I'll hang with you while you eat though."

"I'd like that," he said and sat on the couch. "So how are the edits going?"

"I'm pretty much done. I'm just reading through my changes, then I'll send it back."

"That's great," he said. "I don't know how you do that kind of thing. You amaze me," he said, then took a bite of his sandwich.

"You're the one who amazes me. All these beautiful things you've made? I could never."

He chuckled. "We're both pretty amazing, huh?"

"I think so," I said as I watched him eat. It was impossible to look away.

"What?" he asked, running his hand down his beard. "Have I got food on my face?"

I shook my head. "Nope, I was just thinking even the way you eat is sexy."

A laugh rolled from him, and it was deliciously rough. "Only 'cause I'm on my best behavior with you here. When I'm alone, it's another story completely."

"Food everywhere?" I said, chuckling.

"I'm a pig."

"Do you get lonely?" I asked before I knew I was going to. "It has to be tough out here on your own."

His gorgeous eyes slid from mine and he looked out the window, where it was now sleeting, threatening snow again. "Yeah, I get lonely," he said, then turned to me. "That's why I brought you out here, right? But I was born to live this life. If I didn't like solitude at least some of the time, I'd leave, move to a town or a city." He shrugged. "But that's just not the life I want for myself."

"What kind of life do you want for yourself?" I asked, again before I could stop myself. He'd told me some of this before, over the radio and our calls and emails, but seeing the truth of his words, the depth of feeling right there on his face when he spoke about this place, I needed to see it, I was desperate to see it for some reason.

He flashed me a grin. "This conversation got serious all of a sudden."

"Sorry, I was just—"

"Nah, it's fine." He stared at me for a moment, as if he were deciding what to say. "I think you have an idea."

I did, didn't I? He'd wanted to live out a fantasy where he was married with the woman he was madly in love with, live out here together, have a family. "You want to share this life with a wife and kids."

He blew out a breath and sat back. "I thought I was doing okay, you know? I had my once-a-year visits, my woodwork, my animals to keep me busy. Then Hank met Birdie, and not long after Beau found Freya, then Cash..." He shook his head. "Cash, my stoic, quiet, painfully shy cousin, married Riley. Shit, even he put himself out there and found someone. I saw what they all had together, and I realized I wasn't okay anymore. That I wanted what they had."

"It has to be hard, seeing them all so happy." My heart thundered in my chest. I wanted to tell him it was me, Libby, that I was right here. But now that I saw just how much I'd hurt him, I couldn't do that to him all over again. Learning who I really was, that I'd come here and never told him it was me—he would be devastated. No, it was too late. There was no excuse for my silence. My deception. Even if I'd had no idea it was him I'd be staying with until I arrived, and even if it had been a shock when I got off the plane and my fears had gotten the best of me, it would seem twisted, almost like I was mocking him, or taking some sick pleasure in being with him like this.

Like I was using him.

I'd made the wrong decision and I'd fucked everything up. Ruined everything. Again. There was no explaining this, not now, not after almost two weeks and still not telling him the truth.

"It can be. Honestly, I thought Libby..." He glanced up at me when he said the name, my name, telling me without words something I already knew—she was real, not just some name he came up with. "I'd convinced myself that she was my future. It was naive, just some teenage fantasy to start with. Then she went off to college and we kept in touch, but the emails every week...those emails kept that dream alive, you know? I've never even seen her face. I don't even know what she looks like, I just heard her voice over a crackly radio once a week when we were teenagers, and I'd convinced myself I was in love with her."

My breath caught and I had to force myself to draw breath. "Why her?"

His chin jerked up a little and his brows lowered.

He looked surprised by the question. "You could online date, meet someone, but you haven't, have you? Why?"

He looked back out the window and laughed humorlessly, in a way that was self-depreciating. "I haven't online dated, no, because even though Libs gave up on me—stopped emailing me, stopped answering my calls four years ago—I haven't been able to give up on her. This time, with you, it was my chance to pretend I had what my cousins did, and the only person I could ever see myself with was Libs." He rubbed a hand over his face. "But you're, fuck, you're exactly how I pictured her, Ruth, and the role-playing has got me feeling things I need to stop feeling. I think that last time we played, you worked out where my head was at, yeah?"

"You wanted to punish her for hurting you?" I whispered.

He leaned forward, swallowing thickly, as he rested his forearms on his knees. "Apparently, yeah, I did, and until you came here, I had no idea how fucked up I still was over her leaving me the way she did." He turned to look at me, hurt etched on his face. "For a really fucking long time, she was everything, my best friend, my girlfriend, even if that was only in my damned head, because I truly believed it was inevitable, that Libs and I were inevitable. We shared everything with each other in those emails, well, I did. I've never felt closer to anyone else in my life. When she emailed and said she wasn't where I was, that she needed space and time to think, I guess I thought it was only a matter of time before she reached out to me again. So I decided not to look for someone else. Hiring someone for company was easy, there was no risk of getting attached. Now four years have passed and not a word." He reached out, brushing his thumb over my cheek. "But just so you know, if anyone could make me fall, it's you, Ruth. I really fucking like you. If things were different..." He chuckled roughly and shook his head. "Sorry, that wasn't cool."

"No, don't apologize." I took his hand. When he tried to pull it away, I squeezed it, staring into those gorgeous eyes of his. "Yeah, I..." I swallowed thickly. "If things were different..." I whispered, and said no more, because I couldn't give him what he wanted, what we both wanted.

If things were different and I hadn't grown up in a household full of pain and abuse.

If the idea of living like this again hadn't terrified me so much that I'd stopped emailing and calling because I knew we were inevitable as well.

If only I'd told the truth the minute I got off the plane.

Because, yeah, if things were different—I knew now that I would stay here.

I'd stay right here with Tucker Smith.

❄

It was late when Tucker finally came in from his workshop. I could hear him moving around downstairs. I'd showered and was already in bed.

After our conversation, I'd left him to finish his work and come back in to finish mine. I'd feel even worse that I was doing my own thing on his time, his dime, but he seemed to want space and I needed to keep my mind occupied.

The bedroom door opened and closed carefully before he crossed the room and shut himself in the bathroom. The shower came on next. God, the urge to get up and join him churned inside me so strongly, I almost shoved back the covers and went to him. But I didn't want to push him.

He wasn't in there long though. His tread was light as he moved around the bed, then the mattress dipped when he climbed in. I was facing him, and it was dark, but moonlight streamed in through the window. The patter of light rain, or maybe snow, hit the glass gently. It felt so warm and cozy in his big bed—but he was too far away.

He lay on his back, staring up at the ceiling.

What the hell should I say? Should I say anything at all?

While I did mental gymnastics, Tucker finally turned to me in the darkness, then reached for me under the covers. A shaky breath of relief left me as he pulled me to him. I slid my hands over his broad shoulders. He was naked, his skin hot.

"Need you, darlin'," he said roughly, then he was covering me, rolling me to my back and kissing me.

I wrapped my arms around him, running my hands over his back, over all that muscled, smooth skin. "I'm here," I said against his lips. "Whatever you need, it's yours."

He groaned, his knee slipping between mine as he slid his hand under the T-shirt I was wearing, lifting it, tugging it off and tossing it aside. His hungry kisses moved over my jaw, my throat, then down over my breasts. He sucked a nipple into his mouth, massaging the other one and making me gasp.

"You're so perfect," he said, his hot breath brushing my damp nipple and lifting goose bumps all over me. He dragged his hand down my belly, then tucked his fingers under the waistband of my underwear. "Need a taste of this pussy, darlin'. I'm fucking starved for it."

Darlin', not Ruth, not Libby. I didn't know who he was making love to, but that's what it felt like, like a man making love to his woman. I shouldn't think like that, I needed to stop thinking like that, but my emotions were churning just under the surface. I was still shaken from our earlier conversation. God, I was broken, and so fucking sad at what I'd destroyed, what I'd lost because of my own stupid fears. Tucker would never have stopped me from pursuing my dreams. He would never have tried to control or emotionally manipulate me like my father had my mother, like my father still did. Tucker was nothing like him, something I already knew, of course, but I couldn't deny that was the real reason I'd stopped talking to him. I'd seen a strong woman broken—drained until she was only a shell of herself—for love. Because she believed she was in love. That had altered my chemistry, it had burrowed deep and made it impossible for me to believe in love or to trust easily.

Tucker would have never done that to me. If I'd given him a chance, he would have loved me for who I was, supported me, been there for me. If only I'd shared my fears with him.

He tugged at the front of my panties, and I lifted my hips so he could drag them down my legs. He tossed them aside, before dragging his nose across the soft skin of my lower belly with a groan, then spread my thighs wide and buried his face against my pussy.

My hand flew to the back of his head, threading through his hair. There was agony in his desperate, needy groans. The sounds sent shivers across my skin as he opened his mouth over me, sliding his tongue ravenously across my slick, sensitive flesh. He was tasting and teasing—god, devouring me—showing me just how starved he really was to feel close to someone else.

He took his time, alternating between sucking on my clit and flicking his tongue over it, until I couldn't hold back any longer. I arched against the mattress, fisting his hair tighter and lifting my hips. "Oh fuck...I'm gonna come. *Oh fuck.*" My thighs trembled, and I cried out, rocking against his mouth, biting back my sob. How would I ever be with anyone else after Tucker? I didn't want anyone else.

As soon as I collapsed back, he wiped his mouth on the sheet and rose over me. Taking his cock in hand, he pressed the head against me and, without pause, slid deep, all the way to the hilt.

"*Oh shit.*" I spread wider for him, my hand sliding down his back to grip his firm ass so I could rock up, so I could take him as deep as I could.

He pressed his forehead to mine, his gaze finding and holding me captive as he took me, slow and deep. There was nowhere to hide as he thrust into me, and with every deep glide, he forced a gasp from my lips, and every time he withdrew, I trembled harder. Nothing and no one had ever felt like this.

"What are you doing to me?" he said roughly. "Fuck, Ruth, what the fuck have you done?"

I slammed my eyes closed, hiding the only way I could. I didn't want to hear that name, to be reminded of my lie. I was Libby. I was *his* Libby. His mouth covered mine again then, and he kissed me, as deep and as slow as he was making love to me. All I could do was wrap myself around him and hold on as he slowly yet surely took me with him to the very edge of sanity.

"Fuck," he bit out and shifted his hips.

He slid inside me and stayed there, his thrusts becoming shallow now, so he hit me deep each time. My mouth fell open and my heart slammed wildly in my chest. I dragged my nails down his back, then dug them into his ass as he moved faster, straining against him, gasping for breath.

"Give it to me, baby," he gasped out. "I want to feel you. I need to feel you."

I fell. In every way I could—over the edge, coming for him so hard that I shuddered and cried out—and even more in love with this man than I thought possible.

He groaned, pulsing heavily inside me, his big body shuddering, shaking on top of me.

Then finally, he kissed me again, soft and sweet. "Thank you, darlin'," he said shakily in the darkness. "Thank you."

I held the side of his face, swiping my thumb over his beard and that smooth patch of skin above it that I loved so much. "You don't need to thank me for anything," I said and smiled up at him, hoping in the darkness he couldn't see how close I was to crying.

He stared down at me, his gaze searching mine. Like this, his cock still inside me, his big body surrounding me, this moment felt even more intimate than the slow, tender sex we'd just had, and I couldn't take it.

"I better go pee," I said, then chuckled.

He pressed another soft kiss to my lips, then carefully slid out of me, rolling to the side and letting me out of bed. I took my time cleaning up, but when I came back out, he was still awake. He tossed back the covers for me, and as soon as I climbed back in, he pulled me into his warm arms.

Tucker's breathing evened out a short time later, his arm around me growing heavy as he fell asleep.

I lay awake for hours after, my stomach in knots, because I realized I couldn't leave here and not tell him the truth. Even if he hated me for what I'd done, I had to tell him.

I owed him that.

Even if he never talked to me again.

Chapter Ten

Tucker

"You want tea or coffee?" I called up the stairs.

"Tea, please," Ruth called back.

We'd slept in, then I'd gone down on her because I desperately wanted to make her come again before we finally got up. It was our last day together, and I was doing my best to ignore the dread that was a constant now whenever I thought about her getting on that plane, flying away and never coming back. I knew better than this. I never got attached to the women I brought out here, but this one—she'd dug herself so deep under my skin that all week my stomach had coiled into knots whenever I thought about her leaving.

I had this—fuck—this stupid fucking urge riding me to ask her to stay, to beg her not to leave.

It's only because you've got Ruth and Libby all mixed up in your head.

A ding came from the open laptop on the table. I glanced over at the now glowing screen. A message flashed up from Jessica at the escort service, the woman who organized my visits every year. I shouldn't, but I strode over to take a look. It had to be Ruth's travel times. Jessica always sent them the day before, but I hated to admit that I was kind of hoping there'd been a fuckup with her travel arrangements. That there'd be no one to meet her when Cash dropped her off at the tiny airport at the bottom of the mountain and she'd have to stay with me for another few nights.

Hey Libs,
Just checking in and updating you with your travel times. I hope you're having an amazing time? The girls have all been jealous...

Libs?

Why would Jessica call her that? Was she teasing her? Had Ruth told her the name I'd been calling her while we played? Jessica had always been super professional. It didn't seem like something she'd do, honestly.

My gaze slid to Ruth's script. It was still open, right there. The page was scrolled down so all I could see was the title.

FROM AFAR

I touched the mousepad, using it to bring the front page higher so I could see the rest of it.

Written by
Libby Brantford

I blinked down at the name, then fucking jerked back like I'd been struck by lightning.

What the fuck?

I read it again, and again, my brain struggling to understand, to process what the fuck I was looking at.

Libby Brantford.

Libby *fucking* Brantford.

No. I straightened, then leaned back and read it again. Then I clicked open the message from Jessica so it filled the screen, so I could scroll through their past messages. Her name was all over them, not just from while she was here with me, but from weeks ago. I kept scrolling—fucking months ago.

Her light tread reached me as she came down the stairs, and I turned when she reached the bottom.

She stared back at me, her eyes sparkling, but the longer she looked at me, the more her smile slipped. Her eyes slid to the laptop behind me, then shot back to me.

"Libby?" I choked out.

Her eyes flared, then she stepped toward me, her hands lifted like she was approaching a wild animal, or maybe a skittish one that was about to bolt.

"I can explain—"

"So it is...it's you?" My voice sounded as wrecked as I felt.

Her slender throat worked. "Yes," she rasped and took another step toward me.

I stumbled back, confused. Fuck, I felt sick. "What the fuck is this? Why would you do this? I don't..." I shoved my fingers through my hair. "I don't understand."

"Tuck," she whispered. "Please, let me explain."

When she tried to step closer, I put the table between us. "Stay the fuck where you are," I growled, betrayal and humiliation flooding me. "Was this some twisted joke to you? You cut me off four years ago, then you come out here because what? You wanted to know what it was like to fuck me? Is that it? Are you that hard up in the city that you thought, I know what, I'll go visit Tucker, pretend I'm someone else and see if I can fuck him up more than I already have?"

"Tuck, no, please, you have to listen to me. I had no idea who I was coming to stay with—"

"Bullshit," I roared.

She froze, staring at me wide-eyed, and it took everything in me not to apologize for raising my voice at her. *Jesus fucking Christ.*

"I didn't know it was you," she whispered.

"I don't fucking believe you, Libby. And even if I did, even if that was the truth, you still chose to keep who you are from me this entire time." A laugh burst from me, and it sounded dark, hateful, even to my own ears. "No wonder you got so wet when I fucked you. You must have gotten off knowing just how much you'd fucked me up. God, you must have thought I was pathetic. That's what all those questions were about when we were in the workshop, right? You must have loved knowing I was still hung up on you so badly that I hired someone to pretend they were you."

"No," she said. "I never thought that. I wanted to tell you, but then you said my name, and I...I knew—"

"Just how much you'd messed with my head?"

"Tucker—"

"Were you afraid of me? Afraid of what I'd do if you told me?"

"No."

"Did you think I wouldn't pay you?"

She crossed her arms and shook her head. "God, no, I don't want your money, I don't—"

"What, then? What was it that made you keep lying to me? If this is all some coincidence, why didn't you tell me who the fuck you are?"

"Because I was scared that if I said who I was, that if I told you that every moment I was here with you, I was realizing what a huge fucking mistake I'd made, that I wouldn't be able to leave, and I had to leave." She shook her head. "I couldn't stay here."

I stared at her, my heart hammering in my chest. It felt like she'd plunged a fucking dagger in it. "Nah, Libs, I'll be the one leaving," I said, then strode out of the house, slammed the door behind me, got on the ATV, and tore out of the yard.

I couldn't believe this was happening, that Libby, *my Libby*, was standing in my fucking kitchen.

That it had been her in my bed this whole fucking time.

No wonder I'd been so mixed up, so drawn to her.

Fuck, I thought it was bad enough when she stopped talking to me four years ago. I'd never gotten over it, how the fuck was I going to get over this, knowing what I did now? The look in her eyes when I made her laugh, when I made her come, the sound of her cries and moans, the taste of her lips, the way she felt when I was inside her, the perfection of sitting on the couch with her and just talking, the feel of her wrapped in my arms while she slept.

And after last night, I knew what it was like to make love to her.

How the fuck did I move on from this?

How the fuck was I going to survive?

❄

Libby

Pushing away from the counter, I paced the kitchen again, my stomach in knots, my heart in shreds. *What have I done?*

The hurt on his face, the confusion, the anger.

I'd made everything so much worse. I'd planned to tell him today, this morning. I'd been practicing what I was going to say while I was in the shower, but it was too late, he'd found out on his own, and now he'd never let me try to explain.

It was nearly midnight. He'd been gone all day, and I was past worrying.

Striding back to the counter, I looked out the kitchen window again, like I had been every few minutes.

The sound of the ATV echoed in the distance. Finally. Thank god, he was okay.

I kept pacing, waiting for him to come inside, but he didn't. Then the light in the workshop came on. Just one, the small window right at the top. I watched, not sure what to do, then the light went off again and everything remained still, quiet, and I realized, he wasn't going to come inside.

I couldn't leave it like this, my heart couldn't take it. It physically hurt knowing I'd caused him even more pain. I wasn't getting on that plane tomorrow with him thinking I'd used him and tricked him and that this wasn't tearing me up as well. I shoved my feet in my sneakers, then ran across the yard. Opening the workshop door on silent hinges, I slipped inside. The large space was draped in gloom, only the glow from the moon coming through the windows to light my way. My gaze slid to the stairs on the other side of the huge space, leading up to the mezzanine. Rounding the table, I made my way over, and headed up.

I didn't announce myself. I wasn't going to give him the opportunity to walk away from me again. When I reached the top of the stairs, I searched the shadows, but there was enough moonlight up here to see the bed, and that it wasn't empty.

"Tucker?" I choked out.

"Go back to the house, Libby," he said.

I shook my head, even though I wasn't sure he could see me. "I'm not going without you."

"You've been fine without me for four years."

It was freezing, so I rushed to the bed, kicked off my shoes, slid off my jeans, and got in with him.

"What the fuck do you think you're doing?" he said, and it sounded like he was talking through gritted teeth.

I wriggled over to his side. "You won't come with me, then I'll sleep here."

"I don't want you here," he said roughly, his voice breaking.

"Will you let me explain?"

His eyes glittered in the darkness when they met mine. "That's not why you're here, Libs."

His hand slid into my hair and he pulled me forward. "You want one last orgasm before you leave me, before you fuck off and go back to pretending the pathetic fuckup in the mountains doesn't exist again. You want my cock? Sure, why not?"

I shook my head. "I don't think you're pathetic, and no, that's not why..." He slid his hand inside my panties, gliding his fingers over my clit and stealing my breath. "Tucker, please, we need to..." He hauled me on top of him.

"What? What do we need, Libby? There's no fixing

what you did. But we're good at this, aren't we? You and me. We're good together like this."

I shook my head. "You're more to me than—"

He took my mouth in a bruising kiss, one hand gripping the back of my head, while the other snaked down and dragged my panties aside. The head of his cock prodded me, notching at my opening.

I gasped against his lips. "Tucker—"

"Go on, take it," he growled. "I can feel how much you want it. You're already fucking dripping. One touch and your pussy's weeping for my cock. Take it, Libby, I know you want to," he said more forcefully.

I did, I wanted him, badly, but not like this, not when he thought I was using him. "Yes, I want you, I've never stopped wanting you, but we need to talk." I tried to move away.

Tucker gripped my hips and lifted his, slamming up inside me.

I groaned and fell forward on his chest, lost instantly to the sharp pleasure, lost to him. Tuck held me there, grinding up inside me over and over.

"See?" he said roughly. "This is exactly what you want. That's why you came out here."

"N-no, that's not why I..."

He slammed back inside me.

I shuddered. "Tucker," I called his name desperately.

"I'm right here, Libby, where I've always fucking been," he said and flipped me to my back.

Then he had me pinned down, my wrists held in his hands above my head, while he drove into me. How could this feel so earth-shatteringly good, when every thrust felt as if he were trying to punish me. When he was fucking me like he hated me, like he wanted to wipe the tenderness of the night before from his mind.

"Tucker," I said again. "L-look at me."

His wild gaze locked with mine and he flinched. "Fuck you, Libby," he choked out. "Why did you come here? Why did you do this to me? You've fucking broken me. Is that what you wanted?"

I shook my head, wrapping my legs around him and lifting my hips to meet his angry thrusts. "I came here because I needed the money. I stayed because it was you. Because I got off that plane and saw my Tucker. Mine."

"You're lying."

I shook my head against the pillow. "I'm not. I didn't know it was you. I didn't even look at that part of the brief until I got to the house with you. I was scared that if I looked, I'd chicken out, and I couldn't chicken out. But then my phone died on the plane before I could read it...then I saw you, and you kissed me, and called me Libs, and I was lost. I was too scared to tell you the truth, and the thought of never knowing what it was like to be with you...when it felt so right to be here...close to you."

His glittering gaze bored into me through the darkness. "You left me alone," he gasped out. "You cut me out of your life."

He slammed into me, once, twice, and I arched against the bed, coming hard around his relentless thrusts. He groaned and pulsed deep inside me, coming as well, then he collapsed on top of me.

We lay there in the dark, the only sounds our panted breaths.

I ran my hand up his back, and he shivered. "I left you alone because I was a fucking coward," I whispered. "Because I loved...I love you, and I was so scared of what my life would be if I gave in to what I felt, that I ran from it, I ran from you."

He lifted his head. "Was the idea of living here with me so fucking awful?"

I cupped the side of his face. "I never told you what my life was really like growing up. You were my escape, Tuck. Your calls every week, your emails when I finally got away and went to college...you were my refuge, you always have been."

He searched my eyes. "I don't understand." He jerked back. "What you said, about your father, you were telling the truth?"

"Yes," I choked out. "My father, he...he hurt us. My mom and me. He hurt us, and there was no escape, no help, nowhere to go."

He made a wounded sound. "I didn't know."

"How could you? I didn't tell you." I ran my hand down his chest, resting it over his heart. "I've never escorted before. Jess, she's my roommate, she was trying to decide who to send to this guy, this guy who sounded so great, who liked women who looked like me, and I...I was desperate for money. My mom, she's still with my father. He's really sick, and she's stuck by him, determined to look after him until the end, but she can't afford his medication and his medical bills, so I do it—for her, not him."

"Jesus, Libs—"

"They were the only example of love I knew, and it was toxic and violent and cruel, and I...I didn't trust myself to get it right. I was so scared I'd end up like her, like my mother, a shell of herself."

"You thought I'd hurt you?" There was an ache in his voice.

"No. I know you'd never hurt me, but every instinct told

me to protect myself, to run, that living up here, living this way, so far from everything..." I shook my head. "I thought if I gave in to how I felt about you, that eventually I'd turn into her, into my mom, that I'd give everything up and I'd become a shell, that I'd lose myself completely and it...it scared the hell out of me. The closer we got, the more afraid I became, because what I saw growing up was rooted in me so deep that the prospect of love terrified me, so I stopped emailing you because I knew I wanted to be with you, but I couldn't see a way forward."

"And I pushed you, even though I knew how you felt about living so remote. I pushed you for more until you ran. I'm sorry, darlin'. Fuck, I'm so sorry."

"You did nothing wrong, Tuck. Nothing. It was my fears that broke us. I was too scared to tell you the truth because if I did, I knew you'd be able to talk me around, and I'd be trapped again, with no escape."

He cupped my face with both hands. "And now? How do you feel now?" He swiped his thumb over my cheek. "Because I'd give it all up for you, Libs. I'd leave here and follow you anywhere you want me to. I would've done it back then, and I'd do it now. You just have to give this a chance. I love you. Fuck, I love you so fucking much. There is nothing I want more than you, and that includes this place."

Hot tears streamed down my cheeks, and he swiped them away, but more instantly replaced them, and a sob burst from me. This man, my god, he was everything.

"Libs? Please, baby, don't cry. Talk to me. I need you to talk to me, darlin'."

I pressed my forehead to his. "I love you, too, Tucker Smith, so much. And I...I'm not scared anymore. I want this, to be here with you more than anything else in this world."

His gaze searched mine. "Are you sure?"

I nodded. "Yes, I'm sure."

"I'll take you to the city whenever you want, darlin', I promise. Anything you want, I'll make sure you have it."

I smiled as more tears fell. "All I really want is to be with you."

"You got me." He pressed a hard kiss to my lips. "Fuck, Libs, you've always had me."

Then he wrapped me in his strong arms and held me tight.

He held me like I was his whole world, and I knew the feeling, because he was mine too.

Epilogue

Tucker

Six months later

The theater was packed, and I wrapped my arm around Libs when I noticed how stiff she was sitting beside me. "Okay, darlin'?"

She looked up at me, her beautiful brown eyes wide, almost alarmed. "I know I wanted to keep this a surprise, but now...I'm scared you're going to hate it."

I frowned. "Woman, I am not going to hate your play. Why the hell would you think that?" I whispered as the lights dimmed to signal the play was about to start. The last six months, from the sale of her script to opening night, she'd kept the details of *From Afar* a closely guarded secret, wanting tonight to be the first time I learned what it was about, so this sudden show of cold feet was a surprise.

Her hand slid into mine, and she was fucking trembling. "Libs?"

The curtain opened, and I glanced up as a little girl strode out on to the stage, her parents screaming at each other in the background.

"Tilly, get your ass back here now!" the father roared.

Libs squeezed my hand again, and I knew instantly that the play was about her. The little girl ran across the stage and the lights dimmed. When they came back up, only one side of the stage was lit, and we were in an office and the little girl was nervously pacing beside an old two-way radio.

It crackled, and hand shaking, she picked it up. "Hello, this is Tilly, over."

"Hey, Tilly, you're speaking to Parker." The lights on the other side of the stage lit up, revealing a little boy. He smiled wide. "But you can call me Park."

I blinked down at the stage, my heart in my throat. The story was about us.

When I turned to her, she was staring up at me, still wide-eyed. So nervous. I lifted her hand, kissed the back of it, and smiled down at her. My new wife visibly relaxed and turned to watch her play.

When it finished and we walked out onto the street, I pulled her into my arms.

"What did you think?" she asked and bit her lip.

"I loved it. The only thing I didn't like was the ending." It ended with Libs breaking things off, with her alone and in pain, because she'd written the play before she'd landed on my airstrip six months ago, before she changed both of our lives for the better.

"Me too," she said and curled her arms around my neck. "But I kind of like it this way. The real ending's just ours."

She was right, but then Libs was always right. I kissed her, and when I finally lifted my head again, she smiled up at me. "Let's go home."

❄

Libby

One year later

The small plane tilted to the side as we made a tight turn, then straightened as Cash expertly lined us up for landing.

I peered out the window, my heart leaping in my chest when I spotted Tuck standing by his truck waiting for me.

The wheels hit the ground, and we bounced along, finally coming to a stop. Tuck was there, opening my door before I'd managed to undo my harness. Sweeping my hands aside, he did it for me, then lifted me out of the plane and wrapped his arms around me in a giant bear hug.

"Missed you, darlin'," he said against my hair, then lifted his head and planted a kiss on me that had my toes curling.

"I missed you too," I said, grinning up at him. Three nights was the longest we'd been apart, and I wasn't in a hurry to repeat it anytime soon.

He put me down, but curled his arm around me, keeping me plastered to his side as we talked to Cash, then waved goodbye as he took off, heading home to his family.

"Have you seen much of our guests?" I asked as he wrapped his hand around mine and led me to the truck.

He chuckled and shook his head. "Not a peep. You were right, it's the perfect honeymoon location." He tucked my hair behind my ear. "How are you feeling?" he asked as he opened my door. "Closing night, that's big."

My play had been running off-Broadway for almost a year. It was a huge success, and I couldn't miss the last show. "It was perfect."

"Sorry I couldn't be there, darlin'," he said, cupping my face.

I shook my head. "You don't need to be sorry. We have a life here as well, and I'm excited to meet our guests."

He chuckled. "Not sure you'll get the chance before they leave tomorrow. Last food delivery I did, I just knocked and left it at the door."

"Why?"

"There were some seriously R-rated sounds coming out of that cottage. I'm not sure it's okay for innocent ears," he said, his hand sliding down to my rounded belly.

"I'll wear a thick jacket to muffle out the sound," I said. "The baby won't hear a thing."

Tuck laughed, and my heart fluttered in my chest. I still hadn't gotten used to how goddamned handsome my husband was, and I wasn't sure I ever would.

"Let's get you home, so I can feed you," he said.

"Excellent plan. Cash only had Oreos, and for some reason, they now taste like sawdust. The baby obviously doesn't like them."

He chuckled again, gave me another smacking kiss, and helped me into the truck.

A few hours later I was full and warm after the bath that Tuck had run for me, and when I walked out of the bathroom, my belly did some swirling when I saw him lying in bed, his hands behind his head, waiting for me.

His gaze slid down my towel-wrapped body, and the blood in my veins instantly heated.

"You miss me?" he asked, his eyes hot, gorgeous.

"You know I did," I whispered.

"Were you a good girl while you were away?"

I bit my lip and nodded. "Yes."

"I've been getting you off at least twice a day the last month, you touch yourself, darlin'?"

I shook my head. "No."

"You want me to make you come, Libs?"

I dropped my towel. "Yes, please."

His nostrils flared. "What do you want, baby?"

"I just...I just want you inside me." I climbed onto the bed and crawled over to him. "I want to feel you moving deep inside me."

He released a ragged breath. "You want to ride your husband?"

I shivered. "God, yes."

His hands slid to my hips as I climbed on top of him. His hard body beneath mine was perfection, and I ran my hands down his tight stomach, marveling at the ridges of his abs.

His fingers flexed against my flesh. "Christ, darlin', you're so fucking beautiful."

I reached down between us, curled my fingers around his hard cock, and took him deep inside me.

Tucker hissed through his teeth. "Fuck, baby."

Pressing my hands against his chest, I swiveled my hips, grinding against him. "You feel so good, Tuck. Oh, god, you feel amazing." I moved faster, riding my husband like I needed to, taking him hard and deep in between wild kisses.

"I missed you so much." I'd only been away three nights, but I'd hated it. I hated being separated from him.

"Missed you, too, Libs," he groaned, then cursed. "Gonna come, you keep riding me so hard, darlin'."

I couldn't stop, I sure as hell couldn't slow. His big, rough-skinned hands slid over my hips, my belly, up to my breasts, and he massaged them with another groan. The veins and tendons in his throat, across his chest, strained as he tried to hold his orgasm back.

He didn't need to, I was already there. Squeezing around him tight, my fluttering pussy stroked his thick cock over and over until I cried out, coming around him and pulling him with me.

Tucker let loose a shout, his hands back on my hips, holding me to him as he ground up, filling me, dragging out my pleasure like he always did.

Not missing how tired I was, my husband quickly sat up, taking my weight, and gathered me in his arms, then laid me carefully on my side.

"Got you, baby," he said as he spooned me, his warm arms holding me to him. "Love you so much, Libs. I love our life, and I love our baby," he said as he kissed my shoulder and slid his hand over my belly.

I rolled toward him and cupped the side of his face, smoothing my thumb over his beard. "I thought I knew what I wanted..." I shook my head. "I can't believe I almost missed this, missed this life with you out of fear." I pressed my forehead to his. "I love you, too, Tucker Smith, so much that I'm not sure how I breathed without you."

"You never have to, darlin', not ever again."

❄

The sound of Cash's plane landing, then taking off again pulled me from my sleep. Our guests leaving from their stay in the cottage. Tuck had obviously slipped out to see them off and let me sleep. I thought about getting up, but instead let myself doze off again.

When I woke next, it was late morning. My trip to the city had taken more out of me than I thought, but I was definitely feeling rested now. My hand slid over my belly. I'd had a good pregnancy so far, but I'd definitely been tired a lot, more than I thought I should. It had been worrying me, but after a visit with my midwife while I was in the city, I knew why.

A wide smile curled my lips as I shoved back the covers, as nervous excitement fluttered through me. I had news for my husband, and I planned to tell him tonight. It had been so hard not to blurt it when I first saw him, but I'd managed to hold it back, but I wanted it to be special.

I quickly showered, dressed, and had just finished brushing my hair when I heard a shriek of delight from outside. I spun to the window, and a huge smile instantly curled my lips.

Tucker stood outside with his cousins, Hank, Beau, and Cash, who had his two-year-old daughter on his shoulders, and all four men were struggling with bunches of pink and blue balloons, trying to tie them to the corners of a gazebo, while the kids ran around draping streamers over everything.

What was going on?

The smell of food drifted up from downstairs, followed by excited chatter.

I knew those voices. There was no containing my wide smile as I headed to the kitchen. I was met with delighted laughter when I walked in on Riley, Birdie, and Freya loading plates with food. They rushed me, all taking turns giving me a hug.

"We couldn't let you get away with not having a baby shower," Riley said.

"When did you get here?" Tucker had kept this a total secret.

"This morning," Birdie said, giving me a sweet smile

and curled her arm around my shoulders. "Cash flew us all in. He's been up and down this mountain four times."

"We're all staying at the guesthouse," Freya said. "And wow, it's stunning. We might have to come more often."

I grabbed her hand. "I'll hold you to that."

They pulled me into the kitchen, then they all grabbed plates, and ushered me out the door.

"Time for food," Riley said.

Freya grinned. "And presents!"

I followed them out, my heart impossibly full. I had only known these women a year, but they'd embraced me with open arms. Now I couldn't imagine life without them in it. I loved them all like sisters. They'd rallied around when my father passed away, and supported me any way they could when my mother decided to sell the farm, and move to the city. Hank, Beau, and Cash had taken turns staying here and looking after the animals while we were away for a month helping Mom sort everything out, and move into her new apartment.

And now this.

When I reached the gazebo, Beau pulled me in for a hug. "Hey, honey," he said.

Cash and Hank were not the hugging type, unless it was their wives and children, but even they both gave me hugs. I was surrounded by examples of what a real husband, a partner, a father should be. These men, my Tucker, were all supportive, loving, strong, yet incredibly gentle mountain men.

My husband curled his arms around me, as our family finished arranging the food and finished putting up the decorations.

He pressed his lips to my forehead. "What do you think?"

"I think it's perfect." I looked up at him. "I can't believe you did this for me."

"I'd love to take all the credit, but Birdie, Freya, and Riley were the masterminds."

My belly fluttering with excited nerves. "This is actually perfect timing."

"Yeah?"

"Time to eat!" Riley called.

Tuck led me to the table.

"I have a bit of an announcement to make first," I said instead of taking my seat. I'd been so tired yesterday, and so happy to be home. I'd wanted it to be perfect, special when I shared my news, and you couldn't get more special than this.

Everyone turned to me and I looked up at Tuck. "You know I had a checkup with the midwife?"

His gaze held mine. "Yeah, you said it all went well."

I nodded. "It did. But there's more."

"More? Do you know if it's a boy or a girl?"

I nodded. "Yes. That's exactly what we're having," I said and grinned wide.

I saw Beau elbow Hank in the corner of my eye.

Tuck frowned. "Sorry, so are you saying boy or girl?"

"Both."

"What?" he said, a stunned look on his face.

"The twin gene is seriously strong in this family," I said and bit my lip. Hank and Birdie had two sets now. First two girls, then two boys, and Beau and Freya had three boys. They'd had twins after they'd had Connor. Cash and Riley were the only ones who hadn't had twins, at least not yet. "Are you okay?" I asked, since his mouth was still kind of hanging open.

"Welcome to the club," Beau said, grinning wide.

"The *What is Sleep Again?* Club," Hank added, chuckling.

A huge smile curled Tuck's lips, then he lifted me off my feet with a deep, rough laugh. "Happy to join," he said, then kissed me hard grinning down at me. "So fucking happy, darlin'."

Also by Sherilee Gray

Rocktown Ink:

Beg For You

Sin For You

Meant For you

Bad For You

All For You

Just for You

The Smith Brothers:

Mountain Man

Wild Man

Solitary Man

Lonesome Man

Lawless Kings:

Shattered King

Broken Rebel

Beautiful Killer

Ruthless Protector

Glorious Sinner

Merciless King

Boosted Hearts:

Swerve

Spin

Slide

Spark

Axle Alley Vipers:

Crashed

Revved

Wrecked

Hellhound Heat:

Bad Demon

Bad Magic

Bad Blood

Blood Moon Brides:

Blood Moon Bound

Blood Moon Heat

The Thornheart Trials:

A Curse in Darkness

A Vow of Ruin

A Trial by Blood

An Oath at Midnight

A Promise of Ashes

A Bond in Flames

Knights of Hell:

Knight's Seduction

Knight's Redemption

Knight's Salvation

Demon's Temptation

Knight's Dominion

Knight's Absolution

Knight's Retribution

Black Hills Pack:

Lone Wolf's Captive

A Wolf's Deception

Stand Alone Novels:

Breaking Him

While You Sleep

About the Author

Sherilee Gray is a kiwi girl and lives in beautiful New Zealand with her husband and their two children. When she isn't writing sexy contemporary and paranormal romance, searching for her next alpha hero on Pinterest, or fueling her voracious book addiction, she can be found dreaming of far off places with a mug of tea in one hand and a bar of chocolate in the other.

To find out about new releases, sales, giveaways and other cool stuff, sign up for my newsletter!

www.sherileegray.com

Printed in Dunstable, United Kingdom

66870631R00068